NAZHIN

KIRENAI FATED MATES

TAMSIN LEY

Cover by The Book Brander

Paperback version
ISBN-13: 978-1-950027-63-7

Twin Leaf Press
PO Box 672255
Chugiak, AK 99567

Dear reader,

Thank you for sticking with me as I stretch my writer wings with this series. I don't usually write first person, present tense, let alone a series of books with overarching timelines. It's been a challenge not to accidentally put spoilers in each book! I never want my writing to stagnate for you, and trying new things is the only way for me to continue to improve my stories. I truly appreciate your understanding and support of my creative process.

Be sure to check out the glossary at the back if you are into that sort of thing. Plus there is a bonus section with descriptions of the alien races you may encounter in this series. Happy reading!

Tamsin

1

NAZHIN

I take another sip of *Lensoran* bubbly, letting the sour fizz linger on my tongue as I watch the blue-green planet called Earth grow larger in the viewport. Two cabin stewards—blue Kirenai like myself who are also in human form—bustle between the shuttle's empty rows of plush red seats, readying everything for the first human passengers. Earth is the most exotic destination in the galaxy at the moment, off limits to unauthorized surface traffic, and I'm the only "guest" currently on board. I pulled a lot of strings to get on this flight.

I'm curious to meet my first human, but that's not why I'm here. My marketing team needs images and data to promote a new line of sensors from my family's company, Demod Industries. This is an incredible opportunity to get rare footage of the strange new planet.

One of the stewards pauses next to my seat. "We're almost ready to land, sir. Can I get you anything else?"

I hand him my glass. "No, thank you."

We'll only be on the ground long enough to pick up our human guests—all female—for the IDA cruise, and I need to double check the atmospheric sensor mounted on the outside of the shuttle before we take off again. The Intergalactic Dating Agency charged me nearly as much for the permits to install my equipment as I had to pay in bribes to get a seat on the shuttle, and the trip will be a waste if the sensor isn't working.

The moment we touch down, I stride toward the hatch and wait patiently while the boarding ramp unfurls. Hot, humid air sweeps in, making me nostalgic for my home on Kirenai Prime, though here it smells of bitter petrochemicals rather than sweet happa fronds. I pause at the bottom of the ramp to take in my surroundings.

Our shuttle is the only vessel on a pad made of some sort of hard-packed aggregate painted with white and yellow lines. A strip of shorn green foliage runs down one side of the landing pad, and crude buildings sit in rows in the distance. I can barely make out tiny figures moving around near the structures, but none approach us.

While the stewards position themselves next to the ramp to await guests, I move to the nose of the shuttle and double check the settings on my company's sensor. Everything is within expected parameters, so I upload the data already gathered before stepping away to take a few look around while I have the chance. The view near the vessel is less than spectacular, but I didn't coordinate any extra time for exploration. I activate the Integrated Circuit Chip embedded in my arm to capture images of a few of the buildings, then bend down to examine an interesting green plant growing from a crack in the aggregate.

The plants on Kirenai Prime are blue or red, so the green fascinates me, as does the fuzzy yellow flower in the center of the toothed leaves. A flying creature with a striped thorax lands on the flower, and more excitement fills me. This will be an excellent piece of marketing material. As the owner of Demod Industries, I have all the latest sensor upgrades for my ICC, so I quickly scan the creature's vitals.

Before I have time to review the results, a grating rumble reaches me from the other side of the shuttle. I move around to see a low, boxy vehicle coming to a stop. A female with red-gold hair climbs out, and I start recording as she engages a steward to take her luggage. He leads her up the ramp, and I swivel my recorder back toward the vehicle.

Three other females are getting out, and a human male is removing luggage from the rear of the vehicle. A female with dark hair struggles to remove an enormous case from the rear passenger door. Her sleeveless blouse and shorts expose pale skin that intrigues me, and I wonder if it's as soft as it looks. My current human form is based solely on holo images provided by the IDA to help Kirenai guests assume a form that will appeal to the human females.

After a moment of recording, I realize she can't budge the box on her own and rush forward to help. "Please allow me to assist."

My *Iki'i* immediately registers warm tendrils of gratitude as she turns to me. “Oh, God, thank you. I almost dropped it.”

Her hazel eyes connect with mine, and I suck in a breath. She’s the loveliest being I’ve ever encountered. Her brown hair glints with auburn highlights and is held away from her face by a silver clasp decorated with pointed stars. An intoxicating smell surrounds her, like the petals of a *malila* flower. I stand there holding one end of the box until she raises her eyebrows. “Do you need another porter to help you?”

Porter? I flush with embarrassment, realizing the other end of the case still rests on the seat inside the vehicle. I pull the case easily from the vehicle, determined to prove I can lift anything she needs, even though I’m not part of the crew.

“Please be very careful,” she says. “This is expensive equipment.”

The case is more awkward than heavy as I hold it against my front and follow her toward the shuttle. I can’t help letting my gaze slide down her back to her pert ass and bare legs. “What sort of equipment, may I ask?”

"Astronomy. I'm writing a thesis on the atmospheric properties of an exoplanet we'll be passing during the cruise."

Beautiful and smart. I'd been on matchmaking cruises before and never found a mate—finding a genuine match is rare for Kirenai. But I'm drawn this female, despite having known her a matter of moments.

We reach the top of the ramp and I wave off the steward who tries to take over. "I've got this."

Inside the shuttle, she turns toward me. "Where can I stow this?"

I blink, then cut a gaze across the cabin. "I'm not sure."

The steward gestures toward the back. "If you would follow me, sir, I can show you."

Her mouth drops open. "I'm so sorry. Are you not part of the crew?"

I should tell her I'm not, but I want to keep helping her. So instead, I smile and say, "I'm here to serve. My name's Nazhin."

"Jennifer," she says, following close behind as I carry the case to where the steward points.

My mind is spinning with all the questions I want to ask her, and my crotch is aching with other needs. I haven't felt so strongly attracted to anyone in ages. After stowing the case, I turn around to find her holding out what looks like a slip of colored paper.

"What is this?" I ask, taking it between two fingers.

"A tip." She frowns. "But I guess Earth money probably doesn't do you much good, huh?"

I chuckle and hand it back. "A tip isn't necessary. Though I'd love it if you'd sit with me for the flight up to the *Romantasy*."

Wariness pings my *Iki'i* as she takes a half-step backward. "Sorry, no. I realize this is a singles cruise, but I'm only here for my research. Thank you, though." Without even a glance back, she turns and sits next to the woman with copper-bright hair.

My *Iki'i* reels as if it just collided with a wall. I don't think anyone has ever dismissed me like that, and my chest aches with an uncontrollable desire to be near her. Should I tell her that my company specializes in high-end sensor design? Certainly she'd be interested in that. Then again, she was very clear that she's not interested in being social.

I settle into a seat a few rows behind her as I ponder my options. She's not even open to getting to know me. How can I pursue her if she won't let me near her? And the longer I look at her, the more the need to be near her grows.

She's here to do research. I glance toward where her case is stowed. I bet she'll need to lug her equipment around and will ask for a porter. All I need to do is to be present whenever she needs a hand. And if she thinks I'm part of the crew, well…

The difficulty will be in keeping the secret long enough for her to get to know me without ever actually lying. And the more I ponder it, the more I like the idea. Smiling to myself, I lean back in my seat. I've always enjoyed a challenge.

2

JENNIFER

My sister, Tamara, and I step off the elevator to discover a maze of fancy velvet ropes winding across the shuttle bay floor between us and the purple rosebud shaped shuttle. For the past three days, I've dodged alien advances and endured tedious soirees. Now, finally, my long-awaited opportunity has arrived. We are about to embark upon an excursion through the ionosphere of exoplanet RAx-P-7—known as the Singing Planet to the rest of the galaxy. I've seen hazy images of it through NASA satellite images, and I'm giddy with excitement over the opportunity to document the atmospheric spectrography up close.

Traveling into space has been my dream since Dad gave me a junior telescope for my eighth birthday. The first moment I viewed the night sky through the eyepiece, I knew I wanted to be an astronomer. But after my lab partner ex-boyfriend stole a year's worth of research and published it as his own, I thought my dream might be lost for good.

Then my twin sister, Tamara, won tickets for this alien space cruise, giving me one last chance at a Hail Mary to complete my college thesis on time. So, while most of the other women on board are here for the hot aliens, I'm only interested in viewing the stars and testing my new app. Nobody on Earth has ever captured telemetry like this before, and I know I'm going to blow my professors away with this thesis.

Ahead of us on the shuttle deck stands a small gray alien in a white crew uniform who looks like he came straight from Area 51. He's talking to a pair of tall, broad-shouldered Kirenai wearing Speedos.

Tamara nudges me with her elbow and points with her chin toward the Speedo-wearing guys as they thank him and enter the empty maze. "Jennifer, look."

I chuckle. "Nice."

Somehow, the aliens have it into their heads that human males wear swimming trunks on cruise ships. Now almost every alien guest we encounter wears them—even when there's no pool in sight. Not that I'm complaining—I never imagined aliens could be so good looking, from the blue Kirenai shapeshifters to the gargoyle-like Khargals. Even the short red aliens called Fogarians aren't terrible to look at if you can get past their abundant red body hair and beards.

"More Bloom sisters! How delightful," the gray alien says. The crew members are fantastic about remembering names and have bent over backward trying to make us comfortable.

The alien at the podium points a thin finger toward the shuttle. "Your other party member is already here. Please have an enjoyable trip!"

"Thank you." I lift the nearest rope and duck underneath it. I want to get to the shuttle and set up my equipment before the good seats are all taken.

Tamara grabs my arm and hisses, "They've set those up for a reason, you know."

I scowl at her. Sometimes I wonder how she and I can be twins when she's such a scaredy-cat, but I adore her anyway. I gesture to the empty maze. "It's not like I'm cutting in front of people."

She clutches her big purse closer, one hand inside it to pet her emotional support dog, Beanie. Our other sisters complained about her bringing the animal, but I know Beanie is the only way Tamara can face stress, so I don't mind.

After a moment of hesitation, she grimaces and ducks under the rope with me.

I give her a proud wink and hurry forward, ducking and winding until I spot our sister, Suzanne, skulking near the shuttle ramp. She has wrapped a pastel swirl scarf around her head and neck, and sunglasses hide the rest of her face. She's been trying to avoid a Kirenai admirer she hooked up with on the first night of the cruise.

But my sister and her shenanigans aren't what draw my attention. Next to her towers Nazhin, the brawny blue porter I met the first day of the cruise. Each time he carries my equipment, he looks a little different. He's completely ditched the Ken-doll haircut so many other Kirenai have and is now completely bald. His eyes have acquired a slight silvery sheen, and he's also developed huge muscles —I assume he's shifting to increase them because he's been hauling stuff all over the ship. Even here, from across the shuttle bay, I can see his biceps straining the short sleeves of his uniform. *I wonder what he looks like in a Speedo...*

Shoving the thought aside, I refocus. This might be a singles cruise, but I'm not here to hook up or even flirt. I've already turned down at least half a dozen aliens, the latest being a jerk at the party last night who tried to tell me women shouldn't have careers.

Suzanne spots us and steps out from behind the porter's broad frame with her hands on her hips. "Where have you been?" She gestures toward Nazhin. "Vin Diesel and I have been waiting for at least ten minutes."

I clench my teeth. She's probably been hitting on Nazhin since she got here. Since her divorce, my older sister is determined to do whatever it takes to have a good time.I try to remind myself it doesn't matter as long as she doesn't interfere with him carrying my equipment, but I don't enjoy seeing her flirt with him, especially when she's so flippant about it. "Be polite," I snap, turning an embarrassed smile toward him. "Hi, Nazhin."

"Greetings." Nazhin picks up my equipment case, arm muscles bulging deliciously. "I reserved an exclusive spot in the viewing area for you and your sisters."

When I asked about reserving seats earlier, I was told it was first come, first served. He must've pulled some strings with his buddies on the crew. I drag my attention away from his gorgeous biceps, prepared to thank him, and find his dark eyes locked on me. My heart flutters into my throat. I never get nervous around men, but he's giving me butterflies. Maybe it's because he's bald—I've always had a bit of a kink for bald men. *Once I finish my research, I should find a way to "thank" him for his help...*

My cheeks heat at the thought, and I scramble for an excuse to turn away. Our youngest sister still hasn't arrived, so I look over my shoulder toward the ropes. All I see are two short red Fogarians and a ghostly pale alien with blue hair moving through the maze. "Where's Bethany?"

Suzanne shakes her head. "She bailed on us. Busy teaching an alien how to bake a birthday cake or something." She lowers her sunglasses and stares at Tamara. "I'm surprised you didn't find an excuse not to come, too. You must really have the hots for this pilot."

"Shh!" Tamara cringes and moves to put us between her and the open shuttle door. "He might hear you."

"I thought you *wanted* to get his attention. Speaking of attention, let's get inside before Kiozhi shows up looking for me." Suzanne spins and hurries toward the ramp.

I hurry after her with Nazhin carrying my gear.

A three-foot-tall gray alien with a big head greets me in the hatchway. "Hello, Miss Bloom. Welcome to the Singing Planet excursion—" He spots Nazhin and my equipment, and his small mouth puckers. "I'm terribly sorry, but you'll have to leave your luggage behind."

"This isn't luggage," I say. "It's my astronomy equipment."

"Well, regardless of the contents, you'll have to leave it here. This flight is for passengers only."

I look over the short alien's head toward the double row of seats near the back of the shuttle. "There's plenty of room for my equipment in front of our seats. It won't take up any extra room, I promise."

"I'm sorry, but I must insist." He turns toward Nazhin. "Please return Miss Bloom's items to her cabin."

My chest tightens. My entire thesis rests on the photometry from this excursion. "I was told I could use my equipment anywhere I liked during this cruise."

The small alien's mouth turns up in what I think is a conciliatory smile, and he raises his thin, bony arm to bring up a holographic image with glowing alien symbols. "I see. Do you have a permit number?"

Permit? Shit. I'd let the aliens put my equipment through a crap-ton of scans to be sure none of it would interfere with their systems, and they cleared me for using the telescope on board the *Romantasy*. But I never thought to ask about using it on the shuttle.

Nazhin nudges me to one side, still carrying my case. The muscles in his forearms are nearly as big around as my thighs, and his shoulders take up the entire width of the aisle. He looks down his nose at the smaller alien with a scowl that could crush rocks.

"Were you not instructed to accommodate the human guests in every way possible?"

The smaller alien blinks his huge black eyes and takes a step backward. "There is no room—"

A third crew member appears in the aisle, a Kirenai this time. He hurries toward us and puts a hand on the smaller alien's shoulder, keeping his gaze locked with Nazhin's. "What's the problem here?"

An emblem is emblazoned on the breast pocket of his uniform, so I assume he must be a supervisor. "I'm cleared to use my telescope on board the *Romantasy.* I didn't know I needed a separate permit for the shuttle. Can I get one now? Please, my entire career rests on gathering data from this excursion."

The two put their heads together and mutter too low for me to hear. Based on the way they glance at me, though, I know they're about to deny my request.

Nazhin, however, doesn't appear to care what they decide. He bulldozes past them into the cabin, heading straight to the seats in the back.

My heart is slamming against my ribs, but I scurry after him. *He's going to get me kicked off the excursion altogether.* I can't afford to lose this opportunity.

When I reach the seats, he's already set the case down near a floor-to-ceiling viewport looking out over the mechanics on the shuttle bay floor. There are four seats here set up like train seating; two pairs facing each other with a small table for beverages between them. Suzanne sits in one of the window seats, watching Nazhin with an appreciative gaze that makes me heat with jealousy. *What on Earth is wrong with me?*

I shake off the feeling and glance over my shoulder toward the approaching crewmen who wear fresh looks of determination.

"Shit," I mutter and squat down to retrieve my spectrometer from the case, shoving it into my cross-body messenger bag. If they make me leave my telescope behind, I might be able to record enough data with the smaller instrument and the app I installed on my sisters' phones to produce a passable thesis.

"What's going on?" asks Suzanne.

I keep my attention on the supervisor, raising both palms to face him in a placating manner. "Can I talk to the captain or pilot or something?"

"I have already taken this as high as I can go." He turns to address Nazhin. "Do you want us to call another porter to return the luggage to Miss Bloom's cabin?"

Nazhin crosses his arms over his expansive chest. "That won't be necessary. Please check your log again for a permit."

"We're scheduled to depart momentarily and—"

Leaning forward slightly, Nazhin repeats, "Check. Your. Log."

I'm startled that he speaks to his supervisor this way, but the other alien gulps and calls up a holograph over his forearm. A second later, he licks his lips and turns toward me. "My apologies, Miss Bloom. You are cleared for your study. Please keep all your equipment out of the aisle."

I can hardly process what he's saying, but heck if I'm going to argue. "I will, thank you."

The previously reticent crew members leave, and I set my messenger bag into the chair facing my sister.

"Well, that was tense," says Suzanne.

I blow out a breath and nod, turning a smile of relief toward Nazhin. "Thanks for backing me up."

The look he gives me ignites the butterflies in my stomach again. "It's my pleasure, Miss Bloom. I'll remain on board in case you need further assistance."

"Please, call me Jennifer," I manage to stammer out. "Can you sit with us?"

Nazhin's silvery eyes are bright as he looks at me. "As you wish, Jennifer."

The way he says my name makes me light-headed, and I put a hand on the headrest of the nearby seat to keep my balance. He sits down in the aisle seat next to mine, and I realize I'm still staring at him.

Turning quickly, I open my case and begin setting up my telescope. It's difficult to concentrate with Nazhin at my back, and for the first time in my life, I think I might prefer looking at a man to looking at the stars.

3

NAZHIN

I watch Jennifer arrange equipment in her case and then aim her primitive telescope toward the viewport with a self-satisfied smile. I've enjoyed helping her with her project, and with the aid of a small bribe to the cruise director, I've been present the few times she's called for a porter. Moments ago, I was even able to secure a last-minute permit to bring her equipment on this trip without her knowing I intervened, though I'm worried her sister may suspect something is up after she saw me use my ICC interface to contact my liaison.

I glance toward Suzanne sitting across from me near the window. I know I'll need to reveal my true identity soon. She needs to hear it from me. If anyone else tells her, I don't think Jennifer will take it well.

Luckily, Suzanne's attention shifts to something in the aisle behind me. "Oh, no. You've got to be kidding."

"What?" asks Jennifer, following her sister's gaze.

I twist in my seat to look as well, worry thudding in my chest. Did something go wrong with the permit?

A Kirenai in a cream-colored tunic and dark-green pants tucked into high boots is striding down the aisle toward us. As shapeshifters, Kirenai are often not recognizable by how we look, so I focus my *Iki'i* senses to identify him. I recognize him as a billionaire playboy named Kiozhi; I've met him a handful of times at parties. He's currently in a human form, as are ninety-five percent of the Kirenai on board, with perfectly even features and thick hair. A wide grin splits his mouth, and it's obvious he's heading straight for Suzanne.

Kuzara, he's likely to recognize me. I try to make eye contact and hush him before he says anything, but he doesn't even seem to notice I'm here. He plops into the seat next to Suzanne. "I hope you don't mind, but your sister traded seats with me."

Suzanne turns her shoulder away from him and crosses her arms. “I absolutely do—”

The intercom interrupts the rest of her words. “We’ve closed the hatch and are preparing to take off. Please remain seated until we clear the docking bay doors.”

Jennifer perches on the edge of her seat, one hand holding tight to a leg of the tripod. “Shit, I didn’t think about turbulence,” she says, leaning down to look around the floor. “Is there a way to secure this to the deck?”

I wrap my fingers around the tripod so my hand brushes hers. Her skin is slightly chilly, and I long to take her fingers in mine and share my warmth. Instead, I say, “It’s unlikely we’ll experience turbulence, but I’m happy to hold this in place for you.”

She frowns, her hand stuck like glue to the tripod. Yet her pupils are dilated as she looks at me, and my *Iki'i* can sense her attraction. She’s been looking at me with increasing interest, and my form has been subtly shifting into this strong, hairless build to please her. “Oh, no, I’ll hang onto it,” she says. “You’ve done so much for me already.”

"It's nothing, really." I want so badly to close the distance and kiss her plump lips, but I keep myself in check. Once I've helped her complete her research, I'll reveal myself. By then, she'll understand that I only want the best for her. "You need to be free to take notes."

She inhales slowly, her eyes dark pools of appreciation. "Are you sure?"

"Absolutely."

"Thank you, Nazhin." She releases her grip, but instead of simply withdrawing, she rests her fingertips briefly on my forearm.

A thrill races through me at her touch, and I stare at her pale fingers against my blue skin. I want to lift them to my mouth and suck each digit gently. To kiss her palm and slide my lips up the gentle curve of her arm to her collarbone.

I'm jarred from my daydream by Kiozhi's voice. "Hey, I know you, right? Nazhin?" He leans forward to stare at me, though I know his *Iki'i* doesn't require it. "You own Demod Industries."

Kuzara. This is not how I want Jennifer to learn the truth. I'm proud that I haven't outright lied to her, only allowed her to believe what she sees. But if I deny Kiozhi, it will be a lie, and I never want that to be something she can hold against me.

I clear my throat, deciding the best course of action is to answer his question with another. "Why would the owner of a corporation need to work as a porter?"

I let my eyes flick meaningfully toward Jennifer, hoping she doesn't notice, but Suzanne is staring straight at me, mouth open.

Kiozhi seems to take the hint and reclines back into his seat, affecting a disdainful expression, though I can sense his admiration through my *Iki'i*. "My mistake. Back to your portering." He leans one elbow on the armrest and edges closer to Suzanne. "Do humans have something against rich guys? Is that why you keep rejecting me?"

"Could you be more full of yourself?" She scowls at him, though the sexual attraction is thick between them. I don't know what their deal is, and I don't care. I'm only grateful that her attention has been drawn away from me.

"What's Demod Industries?" Jennifer asks.

"A company that designs high-end sensor equipment." I keep my voice even. "I believe they're currently the largest manufacturer in the galaxy." It was probably a mistake to add the last bit, but I'm proud of my company, and it's hard not to boast.

Interest sparks in her eyes. "Like astronomy equipment?"

"Certainly," I say. "But I'm afraid humans are not permitted to acquire advanced technology until your planet is no longer on probation."

Kiozhi butts in. "I could probably smuggle you a few things."

"Really?" Jennifer leans forward, eyes full of excitement.

Jealousy rises like a storm inside me. She should be looking at me that way, not him. How dare he offer her gifts from my own company?

Suzanne rolls her eyes. "Don't encourage him, Jennifer."

"Can you get me a sensor that can calculate the Roche limit of a planetary body?" Jennifer asks.

"I'll ask my contact once we get back to the *Romantasy*," Kiozhi says, gaze fixed on Suzanne. "Is there anything I can get you?"

He's obviously doing this to impress Suzanne, not Jennifer, but I still want to punch him in the face. He doesn't even have a clue what piece of equipment Jennifer's talking about.

Just then, multi-colored light dances across the window, and everyone gasps. We turn to the viewport where the outer ring of the Singing Planet has come into view. A braided tangle of brilliant pink, green, and yellow light flows against a backdrop of velvet black space.

Jennifer pats my wrist. "You can let go now, I think. I need to start recording."

I realize I'm still gripping the tripod leg hard enough to make my fingers ache. I let go, and she rises to look into the eyepiece of her telescope. Her luscious backside is aimed at my face.

I glance toward Kiozhi, who's leaning halfway across Suzanne's lap to look out the viewport beside her. I'm still seething about his offer. He shouldn't be the one giving Jennifer gifts.

Nobody's paying attention to me, so I bring up my ICC interface and access my corporate account. I know I'm breaking galactic law, but I quickly arrange to have my company's most comprehensive astronomy kit waiting for Jennifer the moment we get back from this excursion. She'll initially think it's from him, but I'll clear that up after I tell her who I really am.

I just hope the right opportunity presents itself soon, or I might end up ruining everything.

4

JENNIFER

I make one last adjustment to my telescope as we enter the outer ring of the Singing Planet, check that it's synced with the laptop CCD array in my case, then settle back into my seat. Outside the viewport, a storm of white lights streak by, reminding me of a snowstorm in the headlights of a car. Everything's moving too fast for me to see, but after we get back to the *Romantasy,* I can slow down the recording for analysis. Every nerve in my body thrums with excitement, and I feel like my entire life has built up to this moment in time.

I pull my phone from my pocket and verify that it's connected to my other equipment. The app I designed will tether our phones and boost my digital processing power.

"Turn on your app," I remind Suzanne, then look around and realize Tamara isn't with us. Feeling guilty that I didn't notice until now, I ask, "What happened to Tamara? Did she chicken out after all?"

"She got a front-row seat with her lover boy." Suzanne holds up her phone to show me her app is running, then returns her gaze to the viewport, giving Kiozhi a blatantly cold shoulder.

This is the first time I've met the guy she's been trying to avoid, and to be honest, I'm not sure how she can tell him apart from the hundred other Kirenai on board. Then again, I've never been great with faces. Show me a star cluster, and I can probably tell you its name along with seven key attributes, but people? Not so much. I slide my attention toward Nazhin, appreciating that he looks unique. *Unique and hot...*

My thoughts are drawn from my musings as a soft, drawn-out note fills the air and golden streamers of light float through the cabin like fireflies. I gasp, and the other guests exclaim in wonder. I understand the ionosphere is only reacting with the hull to create sound and light, but here in the moment, it feels like magic.

The seat cushion softens beneath me and molds up around my body, pulling me firmly against the backrest. "What the—?"

The pilot's voice comes over the speakers. "This is your captain. I've engaged your chair's safety features. It's normal to encounter some turbulence during this excursion, so please sit back and enjoy this galactic symphony."

Turbulence? I struggle to free my upper body, but the seat has me locked down. A spark of panic jolts through me. I need to secure my equipment. The telescope is on loan from the university, and if anything happens to it, I'll be out twenty grand.

As though reading my mind, Nazhin leans over my legs and grabs the tripod again. "Don't worry. I'll hold on. You enjoy the show."

Gratitude warms my chest. I don't know if the other porters on board are this attentive, but Nazhin's anticipation of my needs impresses me. His elbow brushes my bare knee, the feathery contact sending flickers of heat straight to my core. I can't help imagining his hand leaving the tripod to splay over my inner thigh. Without conscious thought, I widen my knees.

Then I realize Nazhin is looking right at me, a slight smile tugging the corners of his mouth. *Oh, God.* He must've noticed what I just did. My entire body feels like it might burst into flames.

Suddenly, the music against the hull shifts, turning into what sounds like a woman moaning in pleasure. I almost groan along with it.

Still, I'm unable to break my gaze from Nazhin's and I'm aware of a pooling heat in my center and a dampness in my panties. I haven't felt this flustered over a guy since my crush on Toby Harrington during my sophomore year in high school. *And I bet Nazhin's a way better kisser.*

Motes of aquamarine have now joined the gold streamers floating between us, merging into glowing emerald rings. I dig into every reserve of willpower I have and tear my gaze away from Nazhin's sultry, silvery eyes to look at my phone. My app seems to catch and freeze before resuming its scroll of code. Something's slowing it down. Then I realize that Tamara's app isn't connected. Without her phone synced in, I won't be able to capture all the data.

She's probably busy making goo-goo eyes at the hot pilot. But she also knows how important this is to me. I don't want to interrupt her, but I have little choice. I text, *Turn on your app please.*

Just as I hit send, purple and red lights explode against the view screen, coating us in a lurid glow. The music dips into a low, mumbling groan, and the ship jolts as the deck starts to shudder. My stomach lurches, and I glance at Nazhin, who's still holding tight to my telescope. "What's happening?" I ask.

His mouth is a grim line, and he shakes his head. "I'm not sure."

Across from us, Kiozhi has one arm flung protectively across Suzanne's middle. Her knuckles are white on the arm rests. "The pilot wasn't kidding about turbulence," she says, her voice higher than normal.

I still can't sit forward in my seat to help hold my telescope and am more grateful than ever for Nazhin's help. Shoving my phone into my pocket, I grip my armrests as the ship's groaning swells into a monstrous roar.

5

NAZHIN

I clutch Jennifer's telescope as the vibration on the hull crescendoes into a shrieking whine. Something is definitely wrong. The scent of broken foliage and ozone fills my nose, and a storm blasts through the cabin, ripping the telescope from my grip. I automatically harden my matrix as wind and debris pepper my skin, then suddenly remember Jennifer doesn't have that ability. *I must protect her*. Twisting, I reach for her just as the seat locks us down, completely encasing us in a mold of safety foam.

My heart races. The only reason the safety pods would engage is if we're going to crash. I can't see. I can't move. Even turning amorphous would be useless because the pod is designed to withstand the vacuum of space. At least I'm in the adjoined seat, so whatever happens, Jennifer and I will be together.

The foam presses around me, filling every nook and cranny. It holds me completely immobile, but I can tell we are spinning, tumbling toward the planet.

And there's nothing I can do except ride it out.

It feels like we bounce several times before we jolt to a stop with teeth-clacking force. Frustrated and helpless, I wait for the foam to deflate and release its hold. *At least it feels like we're right side up.*

The instant warm, humid air hits my body, I tear myself free and stand to make sure Jennifer is unhurt. "Are you all right?"

"What happened?" Her voice is raspy, as if she's been screaming. Her hazel eyes are huge, and her hair has come free of its silver clip, but she looks undamaged. She sags forward, and I reach down to support her so she can stand.

"We crashed." Clasping her against my chest with one arm, I tilt her chin up so I can see her face. "Please tell me you're all right."

"I think so." Nodding, she stands a little straighter, but loops her arms around my waist, as if needing the support while she gets her bearings. I'm more than glad to give it. I haven't had the opportunity to be this close. Her hair smells like warm rain on *happa* fronds, and her body pressed against mine is thrilling, even if the circumstances are dire.

She inhales softly, leaning closer, and her breasts press deliciously against my chest. "God, I can't believe we're still alive."

Before I realize what's happening, her mouth is against mine. Or is mine against hers? All I know is that her lips are as soft as clouds, and when she flicks her tongue against my mouth, she tastes like sugary *kazhitu*. For a flickering moment, I lose myself in the sensation and sweep my tongue against hers, deepening the kiss. My cock throbs with need.

Then I pause. I've dreamed of holding her against me, but not like this, when she feels like a fragile, frightened bird. She's not in her right state of mind, and neither am I.

I gently pull back and press my lips to her forehead instead. My body is at war with itself, demanding I move forward and claim her. But now isn't the time or place. "We should find the others."

She blinks and looks around. "Oh, yes. Where's Suzanne?"

I also glance around the area. Now that my eyes have adjusted, I realize we're standing in a forest of enormous tree trunks. The ground is a tangled mess of roots peppered with bioluminescent plants. Bits of leaves and small branches damaged during the crash flutter down around us like rain. I turn my attention upward. Beyond the faint loops of vines high in the canopy, everything is dark. "The pods must've jettisoned before the shuttle hit the ground and scattered along the flight path. We'll have to search."

A small sob wracks her body. "Do you think they're okay?"

"I'm sure the safety pods protected them." I squeeze her gently. "Can you walk, or do you want me to carry you?"

She sniffles, but says, "I can walk."

Yet her hands remain locked around my waist. Terror, panic, and shock all war for dominance against my *Iki'i*. She needs to focus on something normal so she can reestablish her bearings. Something comforting. I reach up and gently remove her silver hair clip. She's worn the jewelry every day of the cruise, so I know it must mean something to her. I smooth her soft, dark locks away from her face and re-affix the clip. "This jewelry suits you."

As I hoped, the distraction brings her back to herself. She puts a hand to the clip, nostalgia edging into her emotions like a calming tonic. "Thank you. My mom gave it to me. I'm glad it didn't get lost."

On instinct, my fingers glide through her hair down the back of her neck. "I'm glad, too."

Jennifer nods and takes a shuddering breath, her eyes locked on mine. "Thank you for sticking with me, Nazhin. You always seem to know just what to do."

I smile, pleased I've made her happy. But my satisfaction quickly wanes as I realize her equipment is gone, probably destroyed in the crash. "I'm sorry I couldn't save your telescope."

She looks at me with furrowed eyebrows. "Don't be sorry. None of that matters right now. The most important thing is that we find my sisters and the others. Oh, wait!" Pulling her phone from her pocket, she raises it into the air and spins in a slow circle. “I still have my phone.”

“You’ve spoken of this phone before. What does it do?” I wanted to ask when she first brought it up, but the question seemed awkward considering she thought I was just a porter.

“Lots of things. But right now, I’m hoping it will guide me to the other phones.” After two rotations, she drops her arm. “I think I need to get out of this hollow.”

The forest floor is rough and uneven, and our safety pod rests in a wide depression filled with tangled roots. She pulls her bag from where it’s still wedged against the armrest of her chair, then checks around the immediate area for anything we want to salvage. Finding nothing, she leads the way toward the highest spot we can see.

Jennifer stands on top of a tall root and spins with her phone in the air once more. “It’s not working.”

I nod. “I’m not surprised. The planet’s ionosphere is probably causing interference.”

Her shoulders slump. "Crap. I guess we search the hard way, then." Raising both hands to her mouth, she yells, "Hello! Suzanne? Tamara? Anyone!"

We listen, but the only sounds are hoots and crackles, which I assume are normal for this planet's flora and fauna. I help her slide back down the root, and we move through the forest, continuing to call out. The uneven ground is slow going, and we can't keep a straight line. We pause by a pool of inky black water and Jennifer licks her lips. "I'm really thirsty. Do you think it's safe to drink?"

"I can check for known toxins and parasites." I drop to one knee next to the pool and activate the Integrated Circuit Chip on my arm.

For most people, the ICC is little more than a comm device with some data connectivity to the galactic web; mine has several prototype sensors, including one we developed to detect for contaminants after the emperor was poisoned. I've had few opportunities to field test it, and I have to admit I'm excited to see if it's useful.

I lower my arm into the water up to my elbow. A few moments later, I bring it out and read the interface. "Water, some microorganisms which are to be expected, no known toxins." I look at her in triumph. "If we boil it, it should be safe."

One of Jennifer's dark brows arcs in surprise. "Do all the porters have technology like that?"

I hesitate. My ICC is several steps more advanced than what a porter should have. *Kuzara,* with all the sensor upgrades I have installed, it's several steps more advanced than what almost anyone should have. "I need to tell you something." Standing, I shake water from my arm. "I'm... not a porter. I'm the owner of Demod Industries."

She stands there a moment, both eyebrows now raised and her mouth hanging open. I can see the gears turning inside her head. "The company Kiozhi asked you about?" she asks.

I nod.

She crosses her arms, and indignation jabs my *Iki'i.* "The company you very blatantly said you didn't own."

I shrug. "I never denied it. Only asked why such a person would need to work as a porter."

“Yes, that is an excellent question. Why would the owner of a huge galactic tech firm carry around a stranger's luggage for days?”

I rub my lips and move to a nearby root to sit. “When you and I first met on Earth, you made it very clear you had no interest in dating. So…” I swallow, knowing what I have to say but also realizing how bad it’s going to sound. “I had to find another way to get to know you.”

“That’s shady as fuck, you know that?” She spins in a circle as if looking for somewhere else to go. Then she rounds on me. “Why do men always have to lie? I can’t believe I actually kissed you!”

Each word blasts my *Iki'i* like a laser to the chest. This is going worse than I expected. Much worse. “I didn’t mean to deceive you. Really. You’re just so fascinating, intelligent, determined, but also completely walled off—”

“Because I’m not interested in a relationship! What part of that did you not understand back on Earth?”

I clamp my mouth shut. I’m in the wrong here and I know it. Dropping my gaze from hers, I say, “I’m sorry.”

She stands there for a few minutes, seething. Then she turns to the water. "I suppose we're stuck with each other until we find the others. So I sure hope you have a gadget for starting fires on that arm of yours, because I sure as hell don't have a way to boil water."

"No. But I will find a way to start one for you." Despite her anger, an ember of hope flickers inside my chest. We are here, together, with nowhere else to go. I can still prove to her that I'm worthy.

6

JENNIFER

Nazhin's apology blurs my focus on my anger as surely as fingerprints on an aperture lens. I can't recall ever having a man admit he's wrong before, let alone mean it. Yet from the slump of his shoulders to the way his eyes hold mine, I'm certain Nazhin is sincere.

I cross my arms, trying to cling to my anger as I watch him break a thick branch over one knee and tuck the pieces under a well-muscled arm. *Dammit, why does he have to be so hot?*

I have zero interest in another horrible, lying boyfriend. But I also appreciate the way Nazhin has taken care of me. He's been nothing but helpful from the moment we met, caring for my equipment, standing up for me with the crew, and even keeping away suitors who might interfere with my research. I swallow, realizing that last bit of help probably had ulterior motives. *Arthur started out nice, too, and look where that got me.*

Well, Nazhin and I might have to work together until we get off this planet, but I won't let him keep taking care of me. I don’t need a knight in shining armor. Or big blue muscles. All right, maybe his big blue muscles will come in handy, but that’s it. No more letting him coddle me, and definitely no more kissing.

I tromp through the glowing bushes, looking for branches to build a fire, grateful this planet doesn’t appear to have any alien spiders or other creepy bugs. The leaves remind me of nebulas I’ve studied through my telescope—glowing clusters of magenta, gold, emerald, and azure—and I pause to snap a couple of photos with my phone. Might as well have souvenirs of being stranded on an alien planet. Then I bring up my app and turn in a slow circle, hoping I might see the little arrow pointing toward one of my sisters. Nothing. With a deflated sigh, I gather a few sticks and return to the pool.

Nazhin has already accumulated a decent pile of wood, so I kneel and start arranging kindling for a fire. Arthur and I used to go camping to escape the city lights. He would build the fire and set up the tent while I looked at the night sky with my telescope. I assumed he was just being nice and letting me pick what we'd be viewing that evening. Now I know he was simply biding his time and letting me do all the actual work so he could steal it.

"Are you okay?" asks Nazhin, setting down more wood. "You seem… angry."

I look down to see I've snapped the kindling into tiny pieces; the pads of my fingers now prickle with tiny splinters. A surge of self-pity rocks me, and I blurt, "No. My sisters are missing. I've lost tens of thousands of dollars in equipment. And I know this sounds petty, but my thesis is trashed, and I've lost any chance of earning my degree."

Nazhin sits on the ground across from me. "Is the Singing Planet the one you wanted to research?"

I laugh, a bitter, humorless sound. "Yeah, just not quite this up close and personal."

He chuckles, too, and soon we are both laughing hysterically. Tears leak from my eyes, and I lay back on the uneven ground, belly aching.

"Hello?" A male voice calls through the trees.

My laughter chokes off and I scramble to my feet. "Hey! We're over here!"

A Fogarian—one of the dwarf-like aliens from the cruise—emerges from among the glowing bushes, his shock of crimson hair tangled with twigs and glowing leaves. A Ken-doll Kirenai emerges right behind him. They're both wearing Speedos.

I choke back more laughter. *Can this get any weirder?*

The Kirenai looks around. "Are there more of you?"

"No." Nazhin rises. "You're the first passengers we've encountered."

The Fogarian says, "My name is Erud, and this is Handsy."

"I told you not to call me that." The Kirenai looks at me and puts a palm against his bare chest. "My name is Hanzhu."

Erud gives me a sharp-toothed grin that reminds me of a claymation abominable snowman. "You are one of Tamara's siblings, are you not?"

"Yes, I'm Jennifer, and this is Nazhin."

"Very nice to meet you. I'm eager to find your sister. I believe she may be my mate." His eyes burn with hope beneath his bushy brows. This must be the Fogarian Tamara complained about on the cruise.

I give him a sympathetic look. "I think she already has her sights set on someone else, unfortunately."

Erud sighs. "Unfortunate indeed. I direly need a mate." His attention drops to my chest. "Are you available, perhaps?"

Oh, no. The last thing I want is him transferring his attention to me. But before I can form a reply, Nazhin puts an arm around my shoulders. "She is not."

My heart leaps to my throat. I'm not available because I'm working, but Nazhin's arm around my shoulder portrays a different reason. However, I doubt my desire for scientific research will deter Erud's advances. *Nazhin's unspoken hint that we're already together is the easiest way to guarantee Erud leaves me alone.*

Feeling like a complete hypocrite for the deceit, I nod, standing stiffly under the weight of Nazhin's arm.

The Fogarian scowls and crosses his arms. "The IDA should've been more clear about the female to male ratio on this cruise."

Hanzhu points toward the pool behind us. "We should move away from the water. We saw an enormous creature with hundreds of legs come out of a pond like that not too long ago."

Nazhin drops his arm from my shoulder and turns. "I believe this pool is unoccupied. We've been here for some time and detected nothing. Besides, we're going to need a source of water to survive."

Hanzhu reluctantly agrees, and I finish preparing wood for the fire. But without a lighter or matches, I'm at a loss how to start it.

"Please, allow me," Erud says. He scrapes one long claw over a nearby rock, sending sparks onto the tinder, and soon a merry blaze licks up the wood. I have to confess, I'm pretty awed by the ability.

Nazhin rubs the back of his neck. “We don’t have a pan to boil water.”

I pick up an enormous fallen leaf the size of a dinner plate and begin folding it into a cup. “When I was a kid, we used paper cups to boil water on the campfire. Let’s see if a leaf works.”

I fill the folded leaf with water and set it right into the fire. My throat is parched, and if this doesn’t work, I might have to drink straight from the pond. I’m relieved when the water steams and boils. As expected, the top edges of the leaf char and fall away, and getting the cup out of the fire is a challenge, but I lever it out with a pair of sticks. It smells a little like wintergreen and the previously clear water has darkened.

My heart sinks. I never thought about the fact that boiling water in an alien leaf would create potentially toxic tea. “Can you test this again before we drink it?” I ask Nazhin. “In case the leaf is poisonous.”

“Of course.” He dribbles some of the boiled water over his arm. After a minute, he shakes his head. “There are compounds here that aren’t in my chip’s database." Then, without even batting an eye, he downs it in one long gulp.

I grab his wrist. "What are you doing?"

"The only way to test it is for one of us to drink it. If I have no adverse reactions, then it should be safe for you, too."

"I understand the concept, but we should've drawn straws to see who gets to be the guinea pig!"

He tilts his head and frowns. "I don't understand. The cup you fashioned works perfectly well without the use of a straw. And what is a guinea pig?"

I press my fingertips to my temples and take a calming breath. These cultural misunderstandings would be funny if he hadn't just put himself in danger. "A guinea pig is a test subject. The term draw straws means to select someone at random." I gesture to Hanzhu and Erud. "There are four of us now, and we need to be fair about taking risks."

Nazhin doesn't even look at the others. "I'm afraid I can't do that."

"Nor I," says Erud.

Hanzhu shrugs and shakes his head in agreement. "You're female. I'll protect you at all costs."

"Absolutely not," I insist, crossing my arms. I've read enough reverse harem romances to suspect where this might be going, and I have no interest in hooking up with an alien dwarf or a Ken doll. "We're in this together, so we share the risks."

"I agree with what you say," responds Nazhin. "But my physiology is far more resilient than a human's. The risk-reward ratio is greater if I am the kin-ay-peeg."

"Guinea," I correct his pronunciation as I glare at him. Although I want to argue, he has a point. I can't imagine a situation where I might be more resilient than an alien shapeshifter, but it could happen, so I say, "Using that logic, if the risk is lower for me in other circumstances, you let me be the one to take it, right?"

He presses his lips into a thin line and bobs his head once. "After we've considered all other options, yes."

I bite my cheeks and regard him for a moment. He obviously wants to say no, and I have to admit it feels nice to have someone who wants to protect me, but it also feels good to be a productive member of the group rather than a female to be protected. I turn to the other two. "Agreed?"

They glance toward Nazhin before nodding in acceptance.

Nazhin passes more leaves around. "We should boil more water so it's ready for you once we determine I'm okay."

We boil several cups, and after an hour, Nazhin says he feels fine. But now, I'm so thirsty I might consider drinking straight out of the pool. Instead, I sip cautiously at the boiled water. It's a little astringent, but not unpleasant, and hits the bottom of my empty stomach with an aching thud.

"We're going to need a lot more than water to keep us alive if we're stuck here much longer," I say. "How long do you think it'll take for rescue teams to find us?"

Nazhin looks away uncomfortably.

A ball of worry settles in my gut, and I glance at Hanzhu and Erud, who also avert their eyes. "What are you not telling me?"

Nazhin returns his attention to my face, dark eyes somber. "The ionosphere around this planet is nearly impenetrable to sensors. It's unlikely we'll ever be found."

I gape at him, using every spark of brain power to comprehend what he's telling me. I knew the ionosphere was thick, but I assumed alien technology would easily be able to see through it. Dread fills my stomach. *I'm never getting off this planet.* And here I thought my biggest problem was that I'd never finish my thesis.

7

NAZHIN

Jennifer's voice is soft, nearly lost below the crackle of the flames. "Are you telling me we could be stranded here forever?"

"I'm afraid so." I want to pull her to me, but she hasn't forgiven me yet, and the last thing I want to do is make her draw farther away.

"No." She stands up. "I refuse to accept that." She removes her phone from her pocket and holds it up, doing her little circle again. "We're going to find my sisters, then we're going to find a way off this planet."

I can't help smiling. I love her determination, hopeless as it might be. "We'll do everything we can."

Hanzhu rises. "I'm going to rest a bit, then head out to find more survivors." He moves to a thick pile of leaves at the base of a nearby tree and stretches out.

"Same," says Erud. He finds a spot several yards away and uses his clawed hands to dig a shallow depression between the roots. Within a few minutes, he's completely hidden from view.

"That's impressive," says Jennifer, eyeing the hole.

"Yes, Fogarians are skilled excavators." I prefer not to trap myself in a hole in the ground, but I ask, "Would you also like to sleep in a hole like that? I can dig one for you."

"Oh, God, no. I need open air." Jennifer settles down next to me near the fire and looks around. "Should one of us keep watch?"

"Sleep. I'll keep an eye out."

She shakes her head. "You're tired, too. Let's play-rock-paper-scissors for it. Winner keeps watch."

I frown, uncertain. "What is this rock game you speak of?"

Her eyes are rimmed pink, and I can feel exhaustion rolling off her with every breath, but she chuckles. "Right, you wouldn't know what that is." She makes a fist. "This is rock. And this is paper and scissors." She holds her hand out flat, then curls her fingers so only two are extended. "Paper covers rock, rock crushes scissors, scissors cut paper."

I mimic her movements. "All right."

"On three." She counts, moving her hand in time to the beat, and on three holds out paper.

I stare at it, and she laughs again. I grin back. I want to make her laugh all the time. "Now what?"

"You have to do it, too."

"Oh." My grin turns sheepish, and I lift my hand, once more mimicking her.

On three, I hold out a fist. She chooses paper again, and slides her hand over my fist to cover it with her warm palm. "Paper covers rock. I win."

The physical contact, innocent as it is, still sends a thrill through my bloodstream. "Paper can cover rock any time she likes."

Jennifer's cheeks flush pink and her eyes darken. Her hand lingers over mine before she slowly pulls back.

"Uh, so, that means you sleep, and I'll rest after you wake up."

I know I won't be able to sleep, but I lie down anyway and close my eyes. I hear her rustle in her messenger bag and crack open one eye to see her pull out a few gadgets. Her mood is pensive as she looks at one item after the other. I recognize her spectrometer and a compact with a small mirror, but the other items are a mystery to me.

She yawns before stuffing everything back in the bag. Standing up, she stretches and inhales deeply while looking at the surrounding brush. I can tell she's struggling to stay awake, but I doubt I've feigned sleep long enough to claim it's my turn to watch. She paces around the fire, checking on Hanzhu and peeking in the hole Erud dug. Her circles widen as she moves to the perimeter. Her patrol takes her behind the massive trunk opposite to where Hanzhu sleeps. Several heartbeats later, there's no sign of her.

I sit up. During our trek here, she wanted privacy when she relieved herself. Perhaps that's what she's doing now. Except I hear her moving farther away from camp, and she doesn't appear to be slowing down. *Where is she going?*

I get to my feet. We know next to nothing about the Singing Planet's inhabitants, and Hanzhu's mention of a monster has me concerned. She shouldn't venture too far on her own.

"Jennifer," I call.

She doesn't answer.

I move past the tree and call louder. When she still doesn't answer, I lengthen my stride and shove my way through the glowing brush. "Jennifer, where are you?"

"I'm coming!" Jennifer replies, but her voice sounds strangely muted.

I frown and stretch my matrix taller to get a better view over the bushes. She's nowhere in sight.

"We're down here!" an unfamiliar voice reaches me, female and very faint.

Alarm spikes through me, and I move toward it until I reach a shallow crevasse between the roots. The hole deepens at one end, disappearing into a dark cave. I hear movement inside. "Jennifer!" I shout.

"Down here," she calls back. "I think I found someone."

"Wait for me," I call and leap down into the crevasse, moving forward into the darkness. The space is narrow, barely wider than my shoulders, and continues to descend into pitch black. Within a few steps, the passage twists to the right and narrows, forcing me to walk sideways to maintain my human form. I continue on until I see a beam of light. Jennifer stands next to a floor-to-ceiling crack in the wall no wider than my palm. Her cell phone emits a bright incandescence.

"What are you doing?" I ask. "You mustn't wander off alone."

"I heard someone calling for help." She turns to look at me with a puzzled look. "It sounds like they're inside this fissure."

I exhale roughly and grasp Jennifer's arm. "Don't run off like that again."

Jennifer scowls at me and jerks away. "I didn't run off. I was on patrol."

"Can you hear me?" a woman's voice comes from the fissure.

"We hear you," says Jennifer. "Where are you?"

"I don't know. Something was chasing us and we ran and then fell down this hole."

I ask, "How many of you are there?"

"Just me and one of the crew. He's unconscious."

"All right. Don't worry, we're coming." I look at Jennifer. "I'm going to take you back to camp, then I'll come back and find them."

"But I want to help dig them out."

"We don't know what things look like on the other side. Digging might cause a cave in. But I can reach them without disturbing anything." I back up, pulling her along after me. "The best way for you to help is to wait in camp. Boil more water and get ready in case they're hurt."

"Fine. But I can get to camp myself. You need to hurry."

I scowl. "Something chased them into that hole. I'm not letting you go back alone."

Jennifer huffs but follows me. "It's not your job to take care of me, Nazhin. I need you to understand that."

"And I need you to understand that I'll always put you first. I know you're capable, but I couldn't bear it if something happened to you."

Her expression tightens, but she lifts her chin and follows me out. We hurry back to camp where we find Hanzhu and Erud awake.

"What's going on?" asks Hanzhu.

"We found more passengers," Jennifer says. "But we can't get to them."

"I can," I say, giving Hanzhu a meaningful look. He understands immediately that I mean to devolve into my amorphous form.

"Do you want my help?" he asks.

"No," I say. "There's only room for one of us. It also sounds like one may be injured. Get the fire going again and boil more water. I'll be back soon."

I return to the cave where we heard the voice. Releasing my matrix, I squeeze through the small opening. The fissure makes several twists and turns until the space opens up again.

A woman sits on her knees next to a small Hage in a white uniform. Dirt covers her skin, and bits of glowing leaves are stuck in her dark hair. A long tear in her sleeve exposes a plump arm, and the bodice of her red dress is covered in dark spots. Blood? The Hage is on his back, large eyes closed and spindly limbs unmoving. Overhead, I can see the outline of the crevasse they must've fallen through, and crushed, glowing plants and clods of dirt lay scattered on the floor.

I solidify into my human shape. "Are you injured?"

The woman gasps. "N-no." She rises, slightly unsteady. "I'm fine."

"I'm Nazhin. What's your name?"

"Sophia." She points to the unconscious crew member. "He hit his head when we fell."

The Hage's eyelids flicker, and he has a nasty bump on his bald gray-skinned skull, but his pulse is strong, so I think he'll be all right.

"I'm so glad you found us." Sophia clutches her middle, face creasing as if in pain. "First that creature attacked us, then we fell down here. I'm afraid to try to climb out in case it comes back."

I smile reassuringly. "I'll get you out of here, don't worry. We have a camp set up nearby. Tell me about the thing that was chasing you."

Sophia gestures toward the her companion. "Ubi and I were looking for other passengers and sat down to rest. I fell asleep and woke up to something breathing in my face. When I opened my eyes, this… *thing* was on top of me." She cringes, her whole body tightening. "It had pincers instead of a mouth, and wings and scary barbed legs that were wrapped around me like it was trying to carry me off." She runs her hands over the blood spots on her middle, then looks at the crewman, features pinched with worry. "Ubi beat it away with a stick. That's when we ran and fell into this hole. The monster buzzed around outside for a while, but I think it must've been too big to fit through the opening."

She buries her face in her hands.

I pat her shoulder. "It's okay. I don't hear anything now, so I bet it moved on." I look at the opening above my head. "Let me look around up top to be sure."

Sophia clutches my arm. "Don't leave me alone here!"

“We can’t stay here indefinitely. I’ll be right back, I promise.” I gently disengage my arm from her grip. I much prefer Jennifer’s obstinate attempts to be bold over the terror consuming this poor female.

Stretching to my full height, I jump and grab the edge of the opening. I just hope Sophia’s fears are unfounded.

8

JENNIFER

I pace at the edge of the firelight, waiting for Nazhin to return. I never wanted him to be my knight in shining armor, but now that he's out there facing down monsters and rescuing some other damsel in distress, I'm jealous. Not gonna lie.

The moment I hear voices, I bolt in their direction. Above the brush, I see Nazhin with a small, gray Area 51 alien in his arms. Behind him limps a dark-haired woman in a torn red dress. Dirt and blood smudge her perfectly tanned skin and clothes, and she's got one hand hooked into the back waistband of Nazhin's pants.

White-hot jealousy blurs my vision, and I grit my teeth. He's not mine. I shouldn't want him. Yet I can't help the relief flooding my chest. I rush forward.

"You made it! I was getting worried." I force a smile at the woman. "Hi, I'm Jennifer."

"Sophia," she says, coming to a stop so close to Nazhin, her breasts smash against his back.

I loop an arm through hers. "Come meet the others," I say, tugging her away from Nazhin. "We have a nice fire and drinking water."

She looks over her shoulder as we move away. "Thank you so much for coming to my rescue, Nazhin. I don't know how I can ever thank you."

Geez. Can she be more obvious?

"Thank Jennifer," he says, his silvery eyes locked on me. "I wouldn't have discovered you without her."

Sophia returns her attention to me. "Oh, uh, yes. Thank you, too, Jennifer." She leans close to whisper in my ear, "Are you two together?"

My stomach churns. I know I should say no, but I don't want her to think he's up for grabs. "He sort of latched onto me from the moment I boarded the *Romantasy*."

"Ahhh." She nods and sighs wistfully. "I've heard the Kirenai can be like that when they find a mate."

I squirm with discomfort at the thought. Nazhin isn't my mate. I mean, the kiss we shared was electrifying, but I need more than chemistry in a relationship. I need trust, and he lied to me. Except that regardless of how we got to know each other, Nazhin has proven to be a damned nice guy. Furtively, I glance over my shoulder and find his gaze locked on me like the Hubble telescope on a starry nebula. Warming shivers ripple through me, settling in places I shouldn't even be thinking about right now. I quickly face front again but can't keep my lips from twisting into a satisfied smile.

We reach the camp, and Erud and Hanzhu hurry over to offer Sophia help—which she accepts with over exuberant gratitude. *Has she no shame?* I swallow back my distaste. For all I know, she could be the last human I ever see, so I need to be gentler with my judgements.

After a round of introductions, we all settle in next to the fire. Nazhin sits next to me, close but not touching, and I'm glad Sophia seems to have decided to focus her attention on Hanzhu for the moment. The unconscious crewman rouses enough to sip water from a leaf cup Hanzhu holds against his lips. Even with the Kirenai propping him up with one arm, the crewman's head wobbles like a POP figurine, and I worry he might topple over at any moment. I prop a piece of firewood behind him to help him stay upright, then stifle a yawn. I don't know how long we've been stranded here, but it feels like days.

But I'm not ready to sleep yet, not when my sisters are still missing. I glance around at our motley group. "How many people were on the shuttle?"

"I counted five females," says Erud.

"What about males?" I ask.

The bushy-haired alien blinks at me. The guy has a one-track mind.

The wobbly crewman, whose name is Ubi, speaks softly. "Counting crew, there were fifteen people on board."

"So that means more than a third of us are already here," I say, trying to sound cheerful. "The pods must not have dropped us too far from each other."

"This is a good place for a camp," says Erud, glancing around the flattened area at the edge of the pool. "I'll start digging shelters."

Sophia shudders. "I prefer not to be stuck in a hole again."

Erud's whiskers droop, and he glances toward the rest of us, as though begging for support.

Hanzhu pipes in, "We can construct shelters out of wood, too."

"I can help with that," Erud says. "My claws are good for many things."

Sophia gives both men an appreciative smile, which makes Erud grin and edge closer to her. Luckily, she doesn't seem to mind.

"What about food?" I ask. Besides how tired I am, my stomach is an empty, gnawing pit.

Ubi pulls a purple orb about the size of an egg from his uniform pocket and holds it out. "I discovered these growing in the forest. Sophia and I have been eating them."

I glance with alarm toward the other woman. "Are you sure they're safe?"

Sophia shrugs. "He says his species can tell if food is nutritious or not. I've eaten several since we crashed, and I'm not dead yet."

Nazhin smirks. "You're lucky he shared. Hage are known for their addiction to food." His smile fades, and he examines Sophia with a critical eye. "But didn't you say your stomach hurts?"

She half shrugs and nods. "Yes, but I think it's just stress. Ubi, your stomach is fine, right?"

"I have no discomfort," the crewman answers. He twists the orb until it splits open, revealing a juicy interior, and offers half to me. "Would you care to try it?"

I reach for it, my mouth already watering, and sniff the fruit's sweet, musky odor. It smells a bit like cantaloupe. I glance at Sophia. She's dirty, scratched, and her eyes look tired, but she's not doubled over or running off to retch in a bush.

"It's probably fine," I say as much to myself as to everyone else and touch my tongue to the juice. It's sugary and mellow, far better than the water I've been drinking, and I quickly slurp out the pulpy inside. My stomach cramps a little, but I think it's because I'm beyond hungry, not because the fruit is poisonous. Just to be safe, though, I shake my head when Ubi offers me the other half. "I better wait to see how my stomach reacts. Let someone else have some."

Erud accepts the challenge and gobbles it up. "I think I saw more of these on the trail here," he says, licking his dirty claws. "Hanzhu and I will go get them."

They leave, and Nazhin stands. "You all should rest. I'll keep watch."

I want to argue that it's still my watch, but my eyes droop and my head spins with exhaustion. *Maybe the food is poisonous after all.* I feel like I'm on a psychedelic camping trip. Or it's just the stress from the day catching up with me. I yawn, my jaw audibly cracking, and lie down. Within moments, sleep overtakes me.

I dream of sitting in my computer chair, lines of code circling around me like the rings of a planet. But each time I try to focus my telescope on a single command, light blinds me like I just tried to point it at the sun. I blink and try again, bouncing from one line of code to the next. With each bounce, the signal gets stronger. My focus gets clearer. Soon I can see... *I can see—*

I wake with a start. *I know how to reach my sisters.* Why didn't I think of that before? I scramble for my phone before I lose the idea in my head. I'll probably have to delete my astronomy data to make this work, but right now, finding my sisters is more important.

"What are you doing?" Nazhin asks from behind me.

"I know how to get a message to my sisters." I get into the backend of my app and start scrolling through its programming. "If I adjust the frequency of my app settings to send radio signals, I can give my phone a longer broadcasting range."

My hip and shoulder ache from where I was laying against the ground, and the fire has died down to coals, so I know I've been asleep awhile even though the ambient light hasn't changed. Worse, my phone battery is down to ten percent, which means my sister's phones are probably just as depleted. I can recharge mine with my power pack, but that won't matter if their phones die before getting my signal. I'm running out of time. "If I can bounce the signal off the ionosphere, it will travel farther."

"But what if they turned off their devices?"

"I used an override code when I installed the app to give me access, and there's always a tiny bit of power feeding the firmware. I can force a notification to pop up even if their phones are turned off. It's similar to how the NSA tracks spies."

Nazhin raises his eyebrows and nods. "You seem well versed in your technology. I run a tech company, and I usually can't keep up with what my development team is doing."

"I studied computer science for a few years," I say without looking up, though my cheeks warm under the compliment. "There isn't much money in astronomy, and I needed a backup to pay the bills."

"Wise. And it seems you're able to combine the two in a unique way. Your employer is lucky to have you."

"It would be nice if I could find a job that let me do that, but it's hard to be taken seriously in this field when you have breasts."

Nazhin raises an eyebrow. "I think your breasts make you even more desirable."

My cheeks feel hot as sun flares right now, and I can't stop from grinning, but I keep working. "Shh. I need to focus right now."

"Of course." Nazhin sits beside me, his muscular shoulder pressed against mine as he watches me work.

I'm a bit self-conscious, feeling clumsy as I try to to program using my thumbs to input the text. Normally, I do this on my computer before transferring it over. But I enjoy having him close, so I don't complain.

I find the lines of code I'm looking for. To implement my plan, I have to delete everything that might require processing power. Once I make the changes, the phone will no longer be able to receive, only broadcast. *Or it won't work at all.*

Hoping I don't royally screw everything up, I edit the commands and reboot my phone.

When I open the new interface, I gulp. All my beautiful astronomy data is gone, replaced by a dark screen with a blinking cursor. My heartbeat feels fragile and fast. If there's a glitch, there's no way for me to know. But, hopefully, my sisters' phones are now displaying a prominent arrow pointing toward my phone.

Mouth dry, I type, *Follow the arrow. Hurry.*

9

NAZHIN

Jennifer lowers her phone to her lap with a sigh. Worry and uncertainty sour her emotions. "I hope I didn't just destroy my app for nothing. I don't even know if they got my message. Being separated from them is killing me."

Concern flares in my chest. "Do human siblings require proximity to remain healthy?"

She gives me a confused look, then laughs. "Killing me is just a saying. I'm not really dying." Then her mirth fades. "But seriously, I really need to do something to take my mind off my sisters."

I can think of several things I'd like to do with her that would help her get her mind off of them, but I don't think she'd appreciate such a suggestion. I'm just glad we seem to be on good terms again. "We can go gather firewood and forage for food together, if you like?"

"That's a good idea." She stands up and brushes dirt off her clothes.

We let the others know we're heading into the forest, then set out. Worried about stumbling into a hole like Sophia and Ubi, Jennifer uses a long branch to prod the matted vegetation ahead of her. I let her lead the way, scratching marks into tree bark to keep track of our route and enjoying the sway of her ass as she walks.

At a patch of brown shelf-like fungi, she pauses and snaps off one the size of her hand. "Can your sensor tell if things are edible?"

"It's designed to detect known toxins and contaminants, but it won't tell us if it's digestible or nutritious. We'll need Ubi for that." I activate my ICC and purse my lips. There's an unfamiliar alert blinking on my screen. "Hold on. I'm receiving a signal."

Jennifer presses against my side to stare at the interface. "You are? From who?"

Then I recognize the text. It's the same string of human symbols Jennifer sent to her sisters. "It's your phone."

"Oh." Her shoulders slump.

I'm not sure if I should, but I put an arm around her and give her a quick squeeze. "No, that's good. It verifies that you're transmitting. Plus, if my unit is receiving it, other passengers with ICC implants might be, too. You might've just found a way to draw everyone here."

She brightens. "I hope you're right."

I grin at her. "I hope so, too."

Looking at the fungus in her hand, she sniffs it, grimaces, and tosses it aside. "Ugh. Don't bother testing that one. It smells like melted tires."

I'm uncertain what melted tires are, but if they smell anything like that specimen, I don't want to eat them, either. We move on, using my ICC to test a dainty yellow mushroom that Jennifer says smells like waffles, some tender stalks and leaves that look promising, and a few things that resemble nuts. My sensor readings say they're not harmful, but that doesn't mean they won't cause gastric distress. We store them in Jennifer's messenger bag to take back to Ubi.

High on a vine circling a nearby tree, I spot more of the purple fruits like Ubi found. I point. "Look."

Jennifer scrunches one eye half shut and follows my gaze. "Do you think you can lift me high enough to get them?"

I could easily stretch myself up and harvest them on my own, but I prefer her suggestion. It means getting to touch her. I kneel on the ground. "Of course. Sit on my shoulders."

Her eyebrows shoot up. "Are you sure? I'm not exactly a waif."

"Nonsense. You can't possibly weigh more than your equipment."

A flush infuses her cheeks. "I'm not so sure about that."

"I am." I bow down. "Get on."

"Fine. But don't say I didn't warn you." Settling her messenger bag's strap across her chest, she climbs onto my shoulders, positioning herself with my head between her legs.

Kuzara. I feel as if I've been drugged as her sweet scent surrounds me. All I can think about is spinning her around and burying my face between her thighs. Tasting her sweet center. Making her moan with pleasure...

I tamp down on my impulsive desires as I slide both hands up the front of her thighs and rise. I can sense she's focused on our task, and I don't think she'd welcome my overtures just now. The back of my neck tingles as her center settles against my skin. She's warm, even through her shorts, and the skin on her legs is softer than I imagined. My cock rises to full attention inside my pants—luckily, she's not in a position to notice.

When I'm fully upright, Jennifer sways, both hands gripping my forehead. "Oh, God." She laughs, the sound both nervous and joyful. "Don't drop me."

"Of course not." I grin and move close to the vine, hands still on her knees. "Can you reach them now?"

"Yes. Hold still." She stretches up and plucks the purple orbs from the vine, adding them to the collection in her bag. Her breasts are soft against the back of my head, and I wrap my hands more firmly over the tops of her legs. My fingers slide higher on her legs, almost of their own accord, until my fingertips are beneath the cuffs of her shorts near the apex of her thighs.

She flexes slightly and stops moving. I reach my fingers higher, and the heat on the back of my neck increases. She still grips my forehead with one hand, and I can sense her breathing becoming more shallow. My *Iki'i* feels slightly drunk on her surge of desire.

"I think..." Her voice is husky, and she clears her throat before continuing. "I think you can let me down now."

My nostrils flare. I don't want to let her go, yet I can't keep her on my shoulders forever. Lowering myself to one knee, I set her feet o the ground and duck out from under her. But when I rise again, I can't force myself to back away. I'm so close, my chest brushes against her shoulder blades.

She remains frozen in place, her breathing still shallow as she clutches the strap of her bag. A small shudder ripples through her, but she doesn't turn around or move away. Encouraged, I lower my face to inhale the fragrance of her hair. "You smell amazing."

She slowly removes the bag's strap from around her neck, then turns to face me, close enough for our breaths to mingle as she looks up into my face. Her attention drifts down my chest to the obvious swelling in my pants. A soft sigh escapes her, and she licks her lips, staring at my crotch.

Kuzara, I want her to touch me.

She takes a step backward, and my heart constricts, certain she's withdrawing. Her back hits the tree trunk, and she looks into my eyes. Her face is flushed, and she licks her lips. Then, ever so slowly, she reaches out and curls her fingers into the waistband of my pants, tugging me forward.

I need no more encouragement. In a single stride, I'm pressed against her body, drawing her against me for a kiss.

10

JENNIFER

I want Nazhin. I want him like I've never wanted a man before. Perhaps it's the stress of our situation. Of not knowing if we'll live or die on this alien planet. But from the moment we first met, he's been fun and supportive, and every time we touch, I can barely think past the hormones flooding my system. If the bulge in his pants is any indication, he feels the same way.

In a single step, he's pressed against me, one hand behind my head, the other around my waist, pulling me against him. His arms are like a fortress around me, protecting me from this scary alien world.

I tilt my head back and open my mouth to his probing tongue, wrapping both hands around his ribs as he plunders my mouth. Every stroke between my lips and teeth sends jolts of growing lust through me and I moan. He's Kirenai, a species rumored to be the best lovers in the galaxy, and this kiss is so much more potent than I ever imagined a kiss could be.

In the back of my mind, a little voice is telling me I'm crazy. I shouldn't be doing this. Shouldn't be letting another man get close to me. But I can't stop. Nazhin feels right, despite our rocky introduction. And I'm sick of always over-thinking every decision. It's time we act on our mutual attraction.

He tastes like ambrosia, and I can't seem to get enough. I run my hands over the solid muscles of his back and ribs, losing myself to the headiness of the kiss. The handful of guys I've been with tended to be thin, more brain than brawn. Nazhin is a bodice-ripper's dream—not only clever, but tall and strong. A guy any woman would swoon over.

My head is swimming as his tongue leaves my mouth to lick down my neck and settle against the hollow of my throat. He swirls it there, pressing me back against the solid trunk of the tree while his cock throbs against my belly. The hand around my waist slides up my ribs, lifting my shirt. With one big thumb, he snags the bottom of my bra, pulling upward until my breasts are free. I lift my arms over my head as he strips off my clothing. The heat of his palm cups my breast, sending shivers of pleasure through my chest and abdomen. Falling to his knees as if in worship, he latches onto an exposed nipple, sucking and teasing until my back arches. I'm on the edge of coming already, and we've barely begun.

"Nazhin!" I gasp as I grip his shoulders, holding myself up while sparks course through me from his touch. The bark of the tree is rough against my shoulder blades as I writhe, and he moves to my other nipple, sucking it into a hard point to match the first.

His hand slides down my belly and flicks open the waistband of my shorts. As his fingers delve into the top of my panties, I tilt my hips toward him, eager for more. He cups my pussy, and I can feel my arousal slicking his fingers. With a final tease of my nipple, he drops to his knees, tugging my shorts down to my ankles. The fingers cupping my pussy slip between my folds, pressing against my innermost folds, and I gasp. Leaning forward to press his face between my legs, he slides a long finger deep inside me while his tongue flicks against my clit.

I'm not usually into oral sex, but this is mind-blowing. My legs tremble, and I grip the back of his bald head for support while his tongue laps my clit, finger working in and out of my wet center. My blood is on fire, my skin hot as he works me toward the edge of release with a talented, twisting motion I can't even begin to describe.

A tidal wave of pleasure fills my center, and I open my mouth on a silent wail, thrusting my hips against him. Pleasure rolls through me in a cascade that leaves me panting.

He continues stroking me until my legs threaten to give out completely, then he rises and sweeps me onto my back among the fallen leaves at the base of the tree. I think he's going to mount me and take his own pleasure, and I'm ready for it. Ready to feel his weight on me and the driving force of his hips against mine. Instead, he lifts my calves to his shoulders and puts his head between my legs again. His breath cools my hot, wet pussy, and I squirm.

"Nazhin, I want you," I whisper.

"Not yet." He crawls up my body and lies beside me, sliding one arm under my neck as a pillow.

I'm aching for more, but he simply gazes at me with his silvery eyes, a smile on his lips. He's making no move to finish what he started.

What's going on? Does he need me to do something? I reach over and try to pull him on top of me. "You can have me, too. I'm ready."

He shakes his head and cups my cheek. "You're too tempting. I'm afraid I'd claim you."

I know what he means—I've read all the literature about Kirenai mate bonds. But at this moment, I'm so drunk on sex, I'm not sure I care if he claims me. And the fact that he respects me enough to stop himself makes me want him even more.

Not this time, I tell myself. I'm not ready to be bound to him. Not yet. Still, I'm dying to see what his pants are hiding. I also don't want to leave him hanging and frustrated. Rolling toward him, I reach for his fly.

His eyes widen, and he remains perfectly still as I open it and reach inside. He doesn't appear to be wearing underwear, and I look down, my eyes going wide at the sight of his shaft. It's heavy in my hand, long and thick and slightly curved with ridges from base to crown, and the tip is slick with pre-cum.

I wrap my fingers around him and press my thumb over the slit at the top, circling the slippery head. He lets out a shuddering breath, and I glance up to see his eyes closed. He's so sexy, all pent-up sexual energy. I watch his face as I stroke him, sliding along his shaft, increasing my speed as his hips thrust in time to my rhythm.

He flings out a hand and grips my hip, back arching, and I squeeze harder, pumping up and down until he grunts and jerks against me. A stream of milky fluid jets out of him, coating my stomach and thighs. When he stops jerking, he pulls me close, pressing his forehead to mine. "Thank you, my *bareshi.*"

"It's the least I could do." I softly brush his lips with mine. "What's a bareshi?"

"It means brilliant one." He pulls me close, so I'm lying on his chest, his arms a warm cage around me. I've never been given a pet name before, and it gives me a warm glow. I'm not sure I've ever felt more content, despite being stranded in the wilds of an alien planet.

I have the feeling if we're stranded here much longer, I may just let Nazhin claim me after all.

11

NAZHIN

My body is sated, but my mating urge remains strong as I cradle Jennifer against me. Her scent lingers around me, and I can still taste her on my tongue. Before too long, my cock hardens again, and though I'm reluctant to break away, I know I must. My mating shaft burns with the need to claim her, and I'm not sure how restrained I can be if we stay naked together.

We get dressed and trace our way back to camp. Sophia is napping while Erud and Hanzhu are out gathering more wood. Ubi is carefully folding more leaves into cups near the fire. "I'll have to try them one at a time," he says, sniffing the leaves and setting them aside. "Just to be certain there aren't delayed complications during the digestion process."

“Of course.”

“Try this one first,” says Jennifer, holding out the yellow mushroom. “It smells good.”

He nods, sniffs it, then takes a minuscule nibble, his mouth puckered into a frown as he chews. “This needs to be cooked to make it edible.”

We build up the fire, and Ubi skewers the mushroom on a stick, holding it over the flames.

I twist open a purple fruit and hand it to Jennifer, then open one for myself.

“Thanks.” She sucks out the juice and makes a face. “Oh, I think this one isn’t ripe or something. It’s bitter.”

I taste mine. It’s sweet with a lingering, almost sap-like flavor, but I’m fairly certain it’s ripe. I hand her the other half. “Here, this one’s okay.”

We eat several as the mushroom sizzles. As it cooks, a rich, savory scent fills the air. Jennifer groans. “Damn, that smells amazing.”

I set another unripe purple fruit aside and eye our dwindling pile. “I hope it’s worth gathering. At this rate, I don't think these will last as long as we hoped."

Ubi pulls the mushroom off the fire and nibbles one edge. "Mmm." He gulps down the whole thing, chewing with relish. "That's good."

Jennifer stares at him enviously. "So it's edible?"

The Hage smacks his lips. "I need time to digest before I know if it'll cause gastric issues."

Her impatience beats against my *Iki'i* like a drum. "How long will that take?"

"I can't say for sure."

She sighs and nods, then flops onto her back to stare upward. "I wish I could see the sky. I don't think there's been a shift between day and night since we arrived."

I lay on my back on the carpet of fallen leaves next to her, close but not touching. Both my cocks are throbbing with need, and I'm wondering if it was a mistake to let myself go as far as we did earlier. All I can think about is her smell and her softness, and it's taking everything I have to keep myself from rolling over on top of her.

Instead, I focus on science and facts. Things Jennifer will be interested in. "The trees on this planet are well over sixteen-hundred of your Earth meters tall. I don't believe sunlight ever reaches the surface."

"Seriously? Mile-high trees?" She sits up and stares at me. "So there's more than just the ionosphere interfering with sensors. There's a bio-mat between us and any rescue crew searching for us?"

I nod, and she lays down again.

"Well, shit," she says softly, hopelessness falling like rain against my *Iki'i*. I don't like her feeling this way, but it's probably best she accepts our fate. I just hope our earlier intimacy is a sign she'll eventually accept me as part of her future.

Hanzhu and Sophia join us at the fire. They sort through the remaining purple fruits, while Ubi retires to a pile of leaves to rest. I let my eyes drift closed.

When I wake, Jennifer's back is against me. From her even breathing, I can tell she's asleep, but she's shivering slightly. I roll over and spoon my body against hers, draping an arm over her hip. Her shivering eases and she sighs. But her nearness makes my groin ache, and soon my cock feels like a fiery rod pressed against the softness of her backside.

She stretches, wiggling her ass slightly, and I can't restrain the groan that rolls from my throat.

Ubi clears his throat from across the fire, and Jennifer sits bolt upright, scooting away with an adorable pink flush staining her cheeks.

"The mushroom appears to be an excellent source of protein," Ubi says, rubbing his belly.

"Oh, good. I don't think those purple fruits agree with me," says Sophia from where she's lounging against a sizeable piece of firewood. Hanzhu and Erud are busy lashing together long poles to form a shelter. Sophia bats her eyes at me. "Can you bring me back some?"

Jennifer rolls her eyes, and I can sense her distaste for the woman against my *Iki'i*. "We'll bring back some, then everyone will know what to look for when they're out gathering food." She puts a subtle emphasis on *everyone*. "Why don't you fold more leaves and boil water while we're gone, Sophia?"

"The leaves make the water taste funny." Sophia sighs and sits up, reaching for the stack of leaves we gathered to fold into cups.

"Well, you're welcome to drink straight from the pond if you prefer," says Jennifer flippantly. She picks up her messenger bag and heads back into the forest.

I follow along behind, glad I marked the trees along the way. Over time, our trails will probably become more apparent, but right now, the brush is still high and it would be easy to get lost. When we reach the mushroom patch, I bend down to pluck the largest one I see.

Jennifer shakes her head and presses the top of the cap. "Not that one. It's gone soft." The indent of her finger remains in the golden brown cap. "See?"

Tossing it aside, I pluck a smaller one. It feels nice and firm. "How about this?"

"Perfect." She puts it into her bag. "We need to be selective in our harvest, though. If these are like Earth mushrooms, we need to leave about half of them to reproduce." She touches several caps before selecting a few and placing them into her messenger bag.

Thinking it might be best if I let her do the picking, I stand and survey the surrounding forest. After all, the creature that attacked Sophia may still be around, and I don't want to be caught unaware. "How do you know so much about fungus?" I ask. "I thought you were only interested in the stars."

One side of her lip curls in distaste. "Arthur liked to hunt for edible fungi. He was always looking at the ground." She huffs, and I feel a jab of her self-recrimination against my *Iki'i* as she mutters. "I was so stupid not to see it then."

"What do you mean?" I ask, not liking this turn in her emotions.

She shrugs. "He was an astronomy major who never looked at the stars. I should've guessed he was after my research all along."

My hands curl into fists at my sides. *How dare someone steal from her?* "Who is this *Arthur*?"

"Ex-boyfriend. Ex-lab partner. Ex-everything." She shoves a cap into her bag with more force than necessary. "He's the reason I have to gather data on this trip." Her self-loathing is like a noxious cloud against my *Iki'i*.

Although I'm glad to hear he's out of her life, I want to pound the guy into the dirt. I'm snapped from my thoughts of retribution, however, by the sound of rustling brush.

"Something's coming." I signal Jennifer to remain still. Her eyes widen, and she picks up a long stick before pressing her back against the tree. She's frightened, but not in a panicky way, which I appreciate. I lengthen my matrix to peer over the brush toward the sound.

A group of furry beings on four legs lope in our direction. And they all appear to be armed with knives.

12

JENNIFER

I grip my stick and prepare to swing as a pack of furry creatures bursts from the brush, chittering and purring. They quickly surround us, staying just out of range. Nazhin stands in front of me, muscles bunched for action, but there's no way he can fend off this many adversaries, even if I help. At first I think we're being attacked by a pack of human-sized weasels with beady eyes and sleek purplish fur. But then they rise to their hind legs, and I see they're wearing belts or harnesses. Their paws appear to have six digits instead of five, and some of them hold crude knives. *Sentient, then.* And aggressive. Even more disturbing, each of the creatures has an erect pink phallus jutting from between his bandy legs.

I shrink back against the rough tree bark. What the hell do they want? I feel like I'm in an episode of Alice in Wonderland on roofies.

Then a familiar voice calls, "Jennifer!"

My heart almost leaps from my chest. I know that voice. "Tamara?" I lean around Nazhin's broad frame to search for her.

My twin sister pushes between the weasel-men, her copper-colored hair tousled and her freckled face flushed. Her clothes are dirty but undamaged, and a few steps behind her is the large-eyed Kirenai pilot from the shuttle. Tears blur my vision as Tamara yanks me into a tight hug.

I squeeze my eyes shut and clutch my sister tightly. The relief singing through my veins makes me tremble. "I'm so glad you found us," I choke out through a sob.

"I got your message." One arm still around me, she draws her phone from her pocket. The screen is dark except for a small green X in the center that signifies she's reached her target: me.

I release my hold on her and take the device in both hands, zooming out and searching for any sign of an arrow pointing toward Suzanne. All I see is my own green marker. "Have you seen Suzanne? She should've gotten the notice, too."

"No. You're the first people from the shuttle Tazhio and I have found." Tamara pushes the phone down, forcing me to look at her. "Listen. I have to tell you something."

"What?" I ask, recognizing the sincerity in her gray eyes. She tends to be over-anxious, but I sense in this case her worry might be valid.

"There's a parasite on this planet that lays eggs in fertile females," Tamara says. "When the eggs hatch, the spawn eats the host from the inside out. You and all the women from the shuttle are in danger."

Alarm spikes through me. "How do you know this?"

She waves a hand toward the weasel beings still surrounding us. "These, uh, people—they call themselves Sheeghr—"

The word sends a buzzing purr through the group, and the Sheeghr wiggle their hips, their pink boners wagging like flagpoles in a parade. I'd be more alarmed if they seemed interested in me, but all their attention seems focused on Nazhin, who's stripped out of his shirt and is sliding his pants down his perfectly rounded ass. And now that I can see Tamara's pilot friend from the waist down, I realize he's also naked as a jay bird.

"Nazhin, what are you doing?" I gape at the two Kirenai.

Tamara shakes me, trying to draw my attention back to her. "It's a status thing. Now listen!"

But I can't stop looking at Nazhin as he puts his hands on his hips and widens his stance, mimicking the postures of the weasel men. His back looks solid as a marble statue, every naked angle and plane of muscle in full definition. The Sheeghr all have hard-ons—does that mean Nazhin's hard, too? From my angle, I can't tell. I gulp, recalling his massive erection in my hand, and force my gaze to swing back to my sister.

"The Sheeghr say the only way to protect yourself is to get pregnant," Tamara continues, completely blasé about the naked aliens all around us.

I blink, trying to decide if I heard her correctly. "I'm sorry, what?"

"Yeah, I know. Crazy. But you need to get pregnant as soon as possible." She cuts a glance toward Nazhin and then leans next to my ear. "Tazhio and I are mated now, so he's off the menu, but maybe your porter can help?"

"He's not a porter," I grumble. Then my attention drops to where she holds a hand flat against her belly. "Wait, did you say mated?"

"And pregnant, yes." She nods and then shrugs.

I frown, concern forming a lump in my stomach. My twin has always been a nurturer, and I knew she was bound to have kids someday, but not like this. And how the hell does she know she's pregnant? It's not like she ran to the store to buy a pregnancy test.

"Tamara, you can't possibly be pregnant that fast. You just met him." My sister isn't dumb, but I've seen how determined these aliens can be when seeking a mate. And I've never seen her crush on anyone as hard as she did the pilot. But we've only been on this planet, what, a day? Two? She knows better than to jump into something as permanent as a mate bond after such a brief interval. Frustration swells inside me, and I glare at the pilot's bare backside. "Are you sure he didn't trick you into this?"

"Of course he didn't! I was the one pursuing him, remember? And I am pregnant. I know it seems unbelievable, but the Sheeghr can sense it. It's part of their survival instincts to ward off the parasite." She grimaces. "If you don't get pregnant, too, the Sheeghr will try to, um, help you out. They offered to have an orgy with me before Tazhio and I were mated."

I look around at the jutting pink penises, my doubts suddenly turning to fear. We're on an alien planet, and I have to accept that the rules are probably different from what I'm used to. "Is that what they're doing now?" I nearly choke on the words as a nearby Sheeghr grins at me, baring a mouthful of blunt purple teeth as he chitters. "Are they offering to fuck me?"

Tamara rubs the back of her neck. "Sort of, yes. But they allow you to choose your partner. They're matriarchal and respect females."

"They don't look like they respect me. They look like they want to jump my bones."

Nazhin turns around, and my insides do a flip-flop. The head of his upright shaft touches the second row of his eight-pack. *Oh, God.* My legs feel wobbly, and a fresh flood of warmth rushes between my thighs. This is possibly the worst moment in history to feel turned on, but I can't look away.

"It seems you don't need to worry," he says, his expression unreadable. "The Sheeghr say you're already pregnant."

I stumble back a step—literally stumble. *What's he talking about?* "Impossible. I haven't had sex with anyone in months." I also have a dermal implant that should be good for another year. My focus is on my thesis and my career, not popping out babies; I'm very careful when it comes to sex.

But then I remember the copious amount of cum Nazhin jetted over my belly not too long ago. I'd read that Kirenai and humans were extremely compatible for reproduction, but...

My mouth falls open and I stare at him, worry flooding through me. "Just jizzing on me couldn't have gotten me pregnant, could it?"

His eyes narrow. "Of course not. But you said you had a boyfriend on Earth."

I frown and shake my head. "I know for certain Arthur didn't get me pregnant."

Tamara clamps my arm in a death grip. Her eyes are filled with terror like I've never seen before. "Have you encountered a flying creature while on this planet?"

"No, I—"

Tazhio wraps a protective arm around Tamara and attempts to pull her away from me. "If there's a chance she's infected," he mutters, "we have to leave her."

My sister shrugs him off, scowling. "I'm not leaving her. Besides, she said she hasn't met a flying creature."

Nazhin comes to my side, arms akimbo, as if he's ready for trouble. Tazhio stares at me, keeping his arm around Tamara. For the first time, I realize she doesn't have her emotional support dog, Beanie, with her. Concern fills my heart, and I glance around just to be sure, but there's no sign of the tiny chihuahua.

She shrugs off Tazhio's arm and glowers at him. I have to admit, I'm impressed—my once-timid sister seems to have grown some balls since we landed on this planet.

"Are you taking birth control?"

"I still have my implant, yes."

Tamara nods thoughtfully. "I wonder if that makes you immune to the parasite."

I almost sag with relief. "That makes sense."

Tazhio is eyeing me warily. "What is this implant?"

"I have an implant that suppresses ovulation, basically making me infertile."

"I bet it keeps the parasite from being attracted to her," adds Tamara.

I nod, hoping my sister is right.

"Is birth control common among humans?" Nazhin asks.

I half shrug. "Considering we were on a singles cruise and nobody wants to get knocked up on a first date, I'd say it's highly likely most of the women are on some form of birth control."

"That's good news." Tazhio's shoulders relax. "It gives us time to locate the others."

I pick up my messenger bag, hoping the mushrooms inside are still in decent shape. "We've set up a camp not too far from here. There are four other passengers already there."

"Wait." Nazhin takes my arm, stopping me from walking away. He looks at Tazhio. "Describe this parasite."

"I haven't seen one, but the Sheeghr say it's big, at least the same size they are. It lives in the canopy and flies down in search of females when it's ready to lay its eggs."

My heart stops beating for a moment. Nazhin's grip on my arm tightens. I can barely force the words out of my constricted throat. "That sounds like the thing that attacked Sophia."

13

NAZHIN

"How can we purge someone of the parasite eggs?" I ask, glancing at the pack of Sheeghr surrounding us. There are too many to count, and it doesn't help that they seem to be in constant motion. I'm relieved Jennifer won't attract the parasite, at least for the time being. Much as I yearn for her to bear my child, her career is important to her, and if we ever get off this planet, I want her to be able to pursue her dreams.

Tazhio shakes his head slowly, his wariness reflecting off my *Iki'i*. "I don't know. The Sheeghr were ready to kill Tamara if she didn't get pregnant."

Jennifer grimaces and grabs my arm. "We can't lead them to Sophia."

I nod and look toward camp. "But if she's going to explode with hungry parasite spawn, the others in camp are in danger. Someone needs to warn them."

"The problem is, we can't seem to lose our friends here," Tamara says, gesturing toward the milling Sheeghr. "Tazhio and I tried when we left their cave, but they insist on tagging along. I think they're curious about us."

Just then, a feral howl echoes through the woods. Everyone startles, and Jennifer steps closer to me. I'm pleased she unconsciously thinks of me as her protector. "What was that?" she asks.

The Sheeghr's chatter turns to low growls. My universal translator has been identifying a few words, but now there are too many voices at once, and I can't catch any of it. A mix of protective anxiety rakes across my *Iki'i* just before every Sheeghr around us takes off on all fours.

My gut churns. They're headed toward our camp.

A woman screams in the distance.

"Shit! They must've found Sophia." Jennifer takes off through the bushes toward camp.

I'd rather she was moving in the opposite direction if there are parasites around, but she's obviously determined to protect Sophia, so I race after her. My longer strides quickly catch up, and we burst into the clearing around the pool together. Sheeghr seem to be everywhere I look, and the morass of emotions filling the area nearly blinds me. I quickly shield my *Iki'i*.

Next to the fire, Hanzhu slumps sideways to the ground as if in a dead faint. Erud and Ubi are already sprawled motionless. Sophia screams and struggles while several Sheeghr bind her to a long pole.

"Stop!" Jennifer shouts, dodging through the crowd toward the other woman.

My heart thunders against my ribs, and I plow forward, ready to kill anyone who tries to harm her.

She tries to shove the Sheeghr holding Sophia aside. "Let her go!"

One of the furry beings twists and pounces on her, driving Jennifer to the ground.

Oh, hell no. Rage fuels my steps as I move forward.

The Sheeghr scatter out of my way, chittering angrily. Something small and hard thunks against my bare chest, followed by another against my thigh. Two Sheeghr near the edge of the clearing are wielding slingshots. They each fire again, hurling prickly yellow objects that barely sting, even without me taking time to harden my matrix.

Jennifer screams, trying to push the Sheeghr off her.

I dismiss the pitiful missiles and grab the being who has her pinned, easily tossing him aside. More missiles bounce off my flank as I help Jennifer to her feet. They're annoying, making my skin tingle, so I take a moment to harden my matrix, then use my body as a shield to keep any of the missiles from hitting her.

The Sheeghr now have Sophia bound to a pole. They hoist her between them, obviously intending to carry her away.

"Stop them!" Jennifer yells.

We're vastly outnumbered, but I try to do as Jennifer asks and reach for the nearest Sheeghr.

My leg gives out, collapsing me to one knee. I can't feel my foot. A strange sort of numbness creeps through my body, and I try to rise, but can't. I can no longer lift my arms. My head dips and lolls against my shoulder, and slowly, helplessly, I topple forward to the ground.

Kuzara. What is happening to me? This is bad. Very bad. Several prickly yellow balls that look like burrs or gigantic pollen granules lay on the ground in front of my unblinking eyes. *The missiles*. Their barbs must be coated with some sort of poison. No wonder they didn't hurt much. Their damage is much more insidious.

What if one hits Jennifer? I need to protect her, but I can't move. The scuffling sounds of battle continue around me. My matrix is almost completely numb, threatening to devolve into my resting state. I can't let that happen, or I'll be as helpless and vulnerable as an infant. I could even die. Forced to direct all my effort into maintaining my human form, I can only listen while Sophia's screams fade into the distance.

Hands roll me onto my back, and Jennifer's worried eyes peer into mine. "Nazhin? Oh, God. What's happening? Are you injured?"

I can't answer. My mouth won't form words. I can't even blink. In my peripheral vision, I watch her hands glide over me, but I can't feel them.

"Don't touch those yellow prickly things," Tazhio says, somewhere behind her. "They'll paralyze you."

Now he tells us? I wish I could grit my teeth. When I recover from this, that cocky pilot is going to get a piece of my mind.

Jennifer looks frantically around us and picks up a huge leaf. She uses it to brush at the missiles still stuck to my skin. Then she puts a palm against my chest, looking at me with pinched brows. I can feel her concern squeezing my *Iki'i*. It's a comfort to know she cares.

Tazhio appears at the edge of my line of sight, looking down at me.

"Will he be okay?" Jennifer's voice trembles as she glances over her shoulder at him.

"I recovered fairly quickly the first time I was hit," he says with a shrug. "But I only took one missile before I shielded myself. He was hit by a lot of them." He radiates slight concern, and I find myself relieved. If he's not worried, perhaps I shouldn't be, either.

Jennifer sits down and cradles my head in her lap. "Don't you dare die on me, Nazhin." Her worry is still strong, but she smiles tremulously. "I was just beginning to like you."

Kuzara, I wish I could smile back.

14

JENNIFER

I remain close to Nazhin while he recovers, relieved when he finally blinks in response to my murmured assurances. I'm more relieved than I like to admit that he's not dead. The emptiness that invaded my chest when I saw his unblinking eyes is a feeling I never want to experience again.

Hanzhu, Ubi, and Erud are already up and moving, and Erud insists we need to go in search of Sophia immediately.

Tazhio shakes his head. "There's nothing we can do for her if we find her. We don't have any medical equipment to remove the parasite eggs."

"But why did they capture her instead of kill her on the spot?" Ubi asks.

"I'm guessing they'll do something with her body to be sure the eggs can't emerge." Tazhio grimaces and closes his eyes tightly. "I'm sorry I got us into this."

Tamara puts an arm around his waist and leans close. "It's not your fault, remember?"

I shudder. I wasn't Sophia's biggest fan, but I don't wish her ill. Hopefully, the fate the Sheeghr deal her is swift. My heart is heavy as I curl up next to Nazhin for a much-needed rest.

I'm half dozing when I hear a familiar barking somewhere in the forest. Sitting bolt upright, I spot Tamara already on her feet, peering between the trees.

"Beanie, come!" she cries.

I glance down at Nazhin. He's still naked from our encounter with the Sheeghr, and I can't help letting my gaze flick toward his well-endowed crotch before focusing on his face again. He smiles at me, and a flush rises to my face while relief also fills my chest. "Hey there. Feeling any better?"

"Yes." His voice is brittle as he struggles to sit up.

I move to help him, but he squeezes my hand and says, "Just hand me my clothes, please. Then you can go see if they need help."

While handing him his clothes, I lean over and give him a kiss. "I'm so glad you're okay."

"Me too." He smiles, though his expression seems weary.

I rise to join my sister, who continues calling for her dog.

In a few minutes, a tiny chihuahua bursts from the bushes, barking and wiggling. He's a bit scruffy, and there's a bare patch of skin on his rear leg, but overall, he looks remarkably well.

Tamara scoops him into her arms and sobs while he covers her face with tiny pink kisses. "Oh, Beanie, you found me. What happened to you?"

Then another voice among the trees calls, "Hello? Tamara?"

My breath hitches. I'd recognize the voice of my older sister anywhere. Both Tamara and I shout, "Suzanne!"

A moment later, Suzanne appears between the trunks, her red-gold hair a tousled mane around her face. Kiozhi, the Kirenai who sat with us on the shuttle, is leaning on her shoulders, apparently having trouble keeping his balance. The pastel scarf Suzanne originally wore around her head is wrapped around her free arm and spotted with blood, but aside from that, she looks okay.

I rush forward, throwing my arms around her. "I knew you'd find us!"

Tamara joins the embrace, squishing Beanie between us. The little dog wriggles out of her arms and runs over to Kiozhi, now sitting among the leaves. Beanie climbs onto his lap.

"Is he all right?" asks Tamara. I'm not sure if she's asking about Kiozhi or her dog. She looks like she might be a little jealous that Beanie left her to go to someone else.

"I'll be fine," answers Kiozhi, petting Beanie's small head. The chihuahua pants, mouth slightly parted in a doggy smile. "But if you see a tall plant with what looks like gold berries on it, stay far away."

"Good to know," I say, and turn back to Suzanne. My relief at finding my sister is turning quickly to excitement to get the beacon up and running. Now that we've found each other, we can focus on getting rescued. "Where's your phone?"

"Seriously, Jennifer? Is your astronomy project all you think about? You have such a one-track mind." Suzanne crosses her arms and glowers at me.

"This isn't about my project." I scowl. "I'm making a rescue beacon."

"That can wait a few minutes," Tamara says, glaring at me before she turns back to Suzanne. "Have you encountered any monsters? Flying monsters, specifically?"

I grimace, realizing the one-track mind comment was on point. Getting off the planet is of prime importance, but if the parasite has infected Suzanne, we need to deal with that first.

Suzanne's eyes got wide. "Oh, God, are there flying monsters on this planet, too? I thought the gargantuan centipede thing was horrible enough."

"So, no flying creatures?" I ask.

"No, nothing like that."

"Oh, thank God." Tamara wraps her in another hug.

I'm glad to hear she's not in immediate danger, and give her a quick squeeze before repeating, "So… about your phone?"

Suzanne shoves her purse toward me. "In there. But I think it's dead."

I pull out her phone. As she thought, it's dead, but my power pack has enough juice left to bring it back.

We return to the fire, and Erud fluffs a stack of leaves next to him, grinning hopefully at Suzanne. Kiozhi glares daggers at him, and Erud's whiskers droop with disappointment. I'm starting to feel sorry for the guy. Hanzhu and Ubi take the hint that Suzanne must be spoken for and politely but distantly offer food and water.

While Tamara explains about the parasite, I move away and sit next to Nazhin, laying all three phones out in front of me. I dig my power pack from my purse and plug in Suzanne's and my phones. Tamara's battery still has a decent charge, so I tap the app on the display to open it.

"Can I help?" asks Nazhin.

I give him a wary glance. Arthur seldom offered to help, and I'm used to doing things on my own.

He's not Arthur, I remind myself. The feeling that thought invokes is good and warm and makes me want to smile. "That would be great." I get my spectrometer from my bag and hand it to him, glad I grabbed it from my equipment case when we first boarded the shuttle. "I'm going to try to increase our broadcast frequency. Watch the meter and tell me when it approaches three megahertz."

He accepts the device. "I don't think that'll be enough to both penetrate the canopy and get through the ionosphere to orbit."

I frown, knowing he's probably right. But I don't think I can boost the signal above three. I look toward the darkness overhead. "What if we climb one of these trees so the beacon doesn't have to go through the biomass? We can tie vines together for rope, figure out something to use as carabiners, and..."

I taper off, realizing I don't even know what all we'll need. Climbing a humongous alien tree is probably a lot different from using a climbing wall, which I've only done a few times as it is.

Nazhin lifts his chin, regarding the dark canopy overhead. "A Khargal could simply fly up."

I don't recall seeing any of the gargoyle-like aliens on board the shuttle, but I was focused on my telescope, not the other passengers. Then I realize Nazhin might be saying he can do it. Kirenai are shapeshifters, after all. "Is that something you can change into?" I ask hopefully.

He nods slowly. "I can, but assuming a form and using its attributes are two different things. I've never flown before."

I chew my bottom lip. He's also probably still weak from being paralyzed. And flying a mile up into the trees is bound to be a lot of work. My gaze shifts to the other three Kirenai shapeshifters now sitting near the fire. "Do you think any of them could do it?"

From the corner of my eye, I see his hands ball into fists on his thighs. "I suppose if one of them has experience flying, they would be a more logical choice."

I sense he wants to be my hero, which I appreciate, but there's more at stake here than his pride. Standing, I approach the group at the fire. The mood is tense, and both my sisters' eyes are red, as if they're holding back tears. I assume they've been talking about Sophia's demise, which makes my eyes prick with tears, too.

I quickly shove my sorrow aside. I can't save Sophia, but there is still a chance for the rest of us. "Everyone, I may have a way to set up a rescue beacon, but we need to position it as high above the canopy as we can." I look between Tazhio, Kiozhi, and Hanzhu. "Do any of you have experience flying?"

"Sure," Tazhio's mouth quirks into an amused grin. "I've been around the galaxy a few times."

"No, I mean physically," I clarify as Tamara punches his arm playfully. "Like as a Khargal."

They all shake their heads no, but Kiozhi offers, "But I'll try if it means a chance for Suzanne to escape this planet."

I feel Nazhin at my back before I hear him. "I'll go."

I turn to face him, my eyes widening as I take in the massive, bat-like wings spread behind him, each tipped with a sharp claw. He has seven small horns like a crown around his bald blue head, and his fingers and toes now end in hooked claws as well. But his eyes are the same, a silvery hue that makes me think of light reflecting off twin moons. *Vin Diesel with wings*. Badass, clawed bat wings that send a delightful shiver down my spine. Who knew wings could turn me on?

"I'll practice flying while you work on the beacon," he says. He flaps his wings once, lifting slightly off the ground, a long tail twitching behind him. His pants are off again, but he's done something with his shapeshifting to make it look like he's wearing a Speedo. He actually pulls off the look, and I catch Suzanne giving me a knowing wink.

"Okay." I nod at him, trying not to look like a drooling idiot as I return to where the phones are charging. I sit down and pick up Tamara's phone again, but it's hard to concentrate on coding when Nazhin's swooping about the clearing and the other Kirenai are shouting advice.

Finally, I think I have the settings right, and look up to realize Nazhin has stopped his practice. He's with the others near the fire. Tamara and Suzanne have their heads together, and it looks like they may be arguing, but I don't have time for sisterly squabbles right now. The longer we wait, the less battery power the phones will have, so we need to get going.

I place all my equipment in my messenger bag and stand. "I'm ready whenever you are."

Nazhin rises and strides over to me, holding out one clawed hand. "What do I need to do?"

I stare in confusion at his outstretched hand before looking back at his face. "Take me above the tree line."

A worried look flashes over his face. "You? I thought I was taking the beacon."

I bite my lip. I guess I hadn't been completely clear about my plan. What if he's not strong enough to carry me? "I have to go with it. I need a reading of the ionosphere to calibrate the transmission frequency."

"I can handle calibrations." He straightens his shoulders. "I do own the biggest sensor manufacturer in the galaxy, after all."

Pursing my lips, I raise one eyebrow. "That may be so, but I'm pretty sure none of your products are programmed in English."

His smirk disappears. "*Kuzara.*" Tilting his head, he gazes upward. "Carrying you… That's a long way to fall if something goes wrong."

My stomach flip-flops. I've been so focused on getting the app working, I never took time to consider the perils involved with flying. But this is the only option I can see to save us. I put one hand on his arm. "I trust you not to drop me."

15

JENNIFER

I hug my sisters one last time and promise to be back soon, then step into the harness we created out of vines to bind me against Nazhin's chest. Not that I think he'll drop me, but Nazhin insists that it's better to be safe than sorry. Can't say I disagree.

I wrap my arms and legs around him, appreciating the solid feel of his body. But I don't have time to dwell on the intimacy of our position as he leaps into the air, pumping his powerful wings to push us up, up, up between the massive trunks. My sisters and the others quickly disappear from sight, leaving me to admire the forest's glowing understory. It's quite beautiful from up here, a patchwork of neon color and texture…

We drop unexpectedly, and my stomach lurches. "Sorry," Nazhin says, pumping his wings harder. "Just getting used to my new center of gravity."

"Don't worry about me." I let out a shaky laugh. "I'm impressed you're flying at all."

He doesn't look at me, keeping his focus above us, and I decide it might be best if I remain silent so he can concentrate.

Before long, we're flying in near darkness. We reach the first layer of the canopy by bumping into it, and my heart races as we drop a few feet. I wrap my arms and legs tighter around him, squeezing my eyes shut.

Nazhin regains his upward momentum and digs his claws into the bark of a massive horizontal limb. After pulling us awkwardly to the top of a long, flat branch as wide as a king-sized bed, he pauses, his chest heaving with exertion.

"That was incredible," I say, breathing hard as well. I feel shaky with nerves, but he doesn't need to hear that right now. Dropping my legs from around his waist, I stand on my tiptoes, hoping to take some of my weight off him. "Do you need to rest?"

Patches of what might be dimly glowing yellow moss scatter the top of the branch, but don't give off enough light to actually see anything. A low, whooshing roar rises and falls all around us, as if the forest is breathing. I have a sudden thought about the Sheeghr mentioning the parasite lives in the trees. *Could one be watching us from the darkness?* My arms tighten around Nazhin's neck.

His arms are still firmly around me. "I can continue. Are you ready?"

I look up, seeing only more darkness. "I wish I'd thought to bring a handful of those glowing leaves. Can you see well enough to fly?"

I feel him shrug. "No, but up is up. And I'm slow enough to move by feel."

If by feel he means bumping into branches, I guess he's right. And we haven't plummeted to our deaths yet, so I'll have to trust him. I wrap my legs around his waist again, breathing in his warm, masculine scent. "I'm ready."

He launches us upward to the next branch. Again and again we repeat the cycle of Nazhin clawing us on top of a branch, pausing a moment to breathe, then taking off again.

The branches grow closer and closer together the higher we go, and the wind grows more brisk. I thought having more branches would mean more wind protection, but it's strong enough to take my breath away. Leaves and other bits of debris sweep by, stinging my bare arms and legs. I don't know how Nazhin can continue exerting himself like he is. Each time we land, I swear our perch feels less steady, and the air feels colder.

We're airborne when I spot the first slivers of pinkish light overhead through the network of interwoven branches. "I think I see sky!"

A gust of wind sets us spinning, and Nazhin's arms tighten almost painfully around my ribcage. It feels like we're in freefall. Voice locked in my throat, I just squeeze my eyes shut and pray. We slam to a sudden stop, knocking the breath from my lungs. It's a good thing I don't get sick like Tamara does, or I'd be yakking all over Nazhin's chest right now.

After a second of terror, I crack my eyes open to see we've landed on yet another branch. My relief is short-lived, however. The wood is hollowed into a small bowl about the size of a compact car and filled with dry leaves. It seems to be sheltered from the wind, though the entire limb creaks and sways.

"Is this a nest?" I ask, heart thundering against my ribs.

Nazhin rests on his knees, obviously exhausted. He glances around. "I'd be surprised if anything made its nest this high. It's pretty cold, and the wind up here is brutal."

Somewhat relieved, I let my legs fall from his waist. He falls forward on top of me into the hollow. Pinkish light from above outlines his wings and the back of his head, catching on his small crown of horns.

"This might be a suitable spot to set up your equipment," he says, breathing hard. "Are we high enough yet?"

I grimace, uncertain, and stare past him toward the branches. "The beacon can probably get through from here, but my spectrometer needs a clear shot of the sky for a proper reading. If our frequency is off, the signal might bounce off the ionosphere instead of reaching orbit."

"Is the spectrometer something I can use for you?"

"Well, yes, but—"

"Then let me do it." He tugs the knot on the harness behind his neck. The vines release, and he sits back on his knees. The sudden loss of his weight on me makes me feel naked and alone. He reaches into my messenger bag, pulling out the spectrometer. "Show me what to do."

Still uncertain about this plan, I instruct him. My weight is obviously becoming a burden, and the increasing wind only makes flying harder. All I need is a reading from the spectrometer and I think I can make the beacon work.

Nazhin listens carefully, then runs through the steps again with me before tucking the device into the harness belt. "I'll be back soon."

Before he can stand, I grab his clawed hand. "Be safe, okay? Come back to me."

He nods, then he's up and away, leaving me shivering and alone in the hollow.

Without him to block it, the wind bites into my skin, and I soon grow chilled. I sit with my back to one sloped edge of the hollow and pull leaves up around me, but I'm shivering from loneliness and worry as much as cold. The pink glow overhead has grown stronger since we arrived, and I assume it must be the planet is rotating into daylight. *God, I miss seeing the sky*. I bet it's glorious.

My stomach growls, and I dig into my messenger bag for one of the purple fruits we brought along and a cooked mushroom. The food warms me, and I sit back to watch the growing light. What's taking him so long? A list of potential tragedies fills my head as I wait. He's blown off course and can't find me again. He freezes to death before he can get back. He falls to his death…

My stomach is in terrible knots by the time Nazhin returns, and I shoot to my feet to grab him in a hug. "I thought something might've happened to you."

"It was rough up there," he says, putting his arms around me. His teeth are chattering, and he's like a block of ice against me. "I lost your spectrometer."

My heart falls, but I shake my head and drag him down into the leaves, pulling them up around us. "That's okay." I'm actually surprised at how okay I am with it. "I'm just glad you came back safely."

"I took some readings on my ICC that you may find useful." He lifts his arm and brings up the hologram, but he's shivering too badly for me to focus on the image.

"Don't worry about that now." I pull his arm back down into our smothering of leaves. "We need to wait until nightfall to start the beacon, anyway, when the ionosphere isn't already zinging with energy from the sun. That's the optimal time to get a signal through, and I'm worried the batteries won't last very long once I turn it on."

"Okay," he agrees and snuggles closer to me.

I wrap my arms and legs around him to help warm him. He's big, and his wings make him seem even bigger. He wraps them around us like a cloak. Slowly, warmth fills the space around us. In the growing pink light, I examine his features. His Khargal horns are interesting, though his face is mostly the same as his human one. Yet I feel as if I'm seeing him with fresh eyes. "We've been through a lot together, haven't we?" I ask, not really needing an answer.

"Our adventures aren't over," he says, his face somber. "It could be a while before we're rescued—if a rescue ever comes at all."

I gulp. He's right. And while we wait, we have to survive the parasite, the Sheeghr, and God knows how many other monsters we have yet to meet.

Heck, if the wind picks up, we might not even make it back down to my sisters alive.

Sudden resolve fills me. *I refuse to die without experiencing Nazhin.* I've been attracted to him from the first moment we met, and that attraction has developed into genuine affection. Maybe something more, though I'm not sure I'm ready to go there yet. But I know what I want right here, right now.

I put my fingertips against his cheek. "Nazhin, I don't want to die without being with you at least once."

He smiles softly and sighs. "I want you, too, Jennifer. But I can't be with you and not claim you, and you've been very clear that you don't want a mate."

I frown and shake my head. "If we die, none of that will matter."

"But if we live, I don't want you to have any regrets." His gaze is intense and gives me flutters deep in my stomach.

I love that he understands me so well. His refusal only makes me more certain that *not* being with him would be one of my life's biggest regrets, maybe even bigger than my defunct career or my stolen research. "You're right," I say. "I don't want a mate, not in the traditional sense of making a home and raising kids. But I do want a partner who is always there for me, who respects what I want, yet also stands firm for what he needs. I want you, Nazhin."

"And what happens when what you want and what I want are completely opposite?" His eyes are wary, but he doesn't pull away.

"I guess we find a compromise." I lace my fingers with his, careful of his claws. "Is that something you can live with?"

As an answer, he cups the back of my neck and draws me toward him for a kiss.

16

NAZHIN

Jennifer's words echo in my head. On some level, I know I should stop now. Push her away before she makes a choice she'll later regret. But I can't bring myself to do it.

Once I take her, once I plant the genetic markers that make her mine, there will be no escaping this bond. And humans don't feel the tie like Kirenai do. If she ignores our union, it could drive me insane. But as my lips move over hers, I'm helpless to deny myself.

She wraps her arms around my neck, pressing her breasts deliciously against my chest. I explore every corner of her mouth, staking my claim as my fingers trace patterns down her shoulders to the base of her spine.

Her muscles shift beneath my touch, and she throws her leg over mine, straddling my hips. The need to be inside her is overwhelming. My *Iki'i* senses she feels the same way as she pulls me tighter against her heated center. When I assumed this Khargal form, I shed my pants so I could make use of my tail while flying, but had adopted a modesty shield to obscure my genitals as humans prefer. Now both of my shafts burst free, pushing my matrix aside to make themselves known.

She gasps as I throb against her, then her hand works its way between us, grasping my primary shaft as she'd done during our previous intimacy.

I hiss, "*Kuzara,* Jennifer. I won't last long if you keep that up."

She pulls back, reaching down to lift the hem of her blouse over her head. Her nipples are already hard, her breasts perfect mounds of softness I can't wait to taste. I lean in and capture one nipple, circling it with my tongue until she arches her back and moans, both hands clutched around my head.

Her thumb runs across the Khargal horns, and I shudder. I nip the stiff bud of her nipple before I slip my hand between us to cup the heat between her legs. She responds immediately by flicking open the front of her shorts. After a moment of contortions, she sheds both shorts and panties. I can wait no longer. I roll her onto her back and position myself between her legs, the head of my shaft poised at her entrance. "Are you certain?" I offer one more time.

Jennifer nods, eyes glittering with heated desire. "Take me."

I enter her slowly, her tight flesh gripping me in exquisite heat and wetness. I have to breathe slowly to keep myself from finishing before we've even started. Once I've sunk completely inside her, I press my tickler against her clit.

"Oh," she growls, her voice filled with a sultry need that makes my blood sing.

Controlling my tickler takes finesse, but soon I have her writhing beneath me as her engorged clit pulses, her juices surging around our joining. She gasps and shudders, and I know it's time.

Pulling out partway, I slam into her again, pleasure driving me like an animal. My mating shaft is pulsing and ready, prodding her ass with every forward thrust. She bucks up to meet me, her breath coming in tiny, panting gasps as our rhythm increases. I feel myself nearing the brink and slow my thrusting, wanting to make it last longer.

She digs her nails into my back. “Don’t stop. Don’t stop!”

Happy to oblige, I thrust again. This time, my mating shaft sinks into her ass. I can no longer hold back, my release rolling through me like lightning. Her inner walls tighten to almost painful strength, her orgasm colliding with mine as we both shudder and moan, the groaning of the wind and trees a counterpoint to our intensity. The pleasure seems to go on for an eternity as I pulse inside her, each shaft filling her and making her mine.

I sag on top of her, my wings spread over us like a protective blanket. Her fingers stroke my lower back and ribs.

“Tell me you’re my mate,” I say. I need to hear her say it.

“I’m yours, Nazhin.” She kisses the side of my neck and along my collarbone. “Your mate.”

I nuzzle against her ear and speak the words I've been dying to say for so long. "I love you, Jennifer."

She makes a soft, happy sound and runs one hand along the inside of my spread wing. "Will it be like this every time? Or only when you're a Khargal?"

Then I realize what has—or rather hasn't—happened. My form isn't settled. I'm not bound as a human. I lift a clawed hand to my forehead and touch my horns. *Curious*. "Most Kirenai assume the male form of their mate's species upon bonding."

Disappointment sours the air. "But you're obviously still Khargal. Does this mean… we're not mates?"

I glance at her sharply. "We are most definitely mates."

"How can you be so sure?" Her eyes are tight with worry.

"My *Iki'i* doesn't lie."

I push onto my knees, letting the wind tug at my wings. "Perhaps it's because you prefer me as a Khargal."

She laughs. "The wings are sexy, but I liked your Vin Diesel form, too. Can you still shift into that one?"

I stretch out my hand and try to retract my claws. Only when I focus all my energy on a single digit can I make the change happen, and the nail quickly resumes its Khargal shape when I stop concentrating. "There are legends about Kirenai who don't assume the shape their mate prefers, but only when the mating is under great duress."

Jennifer reaches for her shorts and panties, which have ended up precariously close to the edge of our perch. "Well, our situation probably qualifies. I mean, if you lost your wings right now, we'd be fucked."

My blood turns to ice. "*Kuzara,* I never even considered that." I'd been too swept up in the moment to consider there might be consequences to our joining under these conditions. "I'd better not try a full shift just yet. Just in case I can't shift back again."

She snuggles against me. "Well, if you can't shift back, I'll take you in whatever form you have to be in. Wings, no wings, whatever."

"That makes me so happy, *bareshi*." I lay down beside her and cover her with my wing.

"What was it like up there above the trees?" she asks. "I bet it was glorious."

"I wish I could take you to see it. The entire sky is an aurora. Lots of red and purple and orange, like a river of sunsets. But the storm..." I inhale deeply, recalling the moment I lost her spectrometer. The wind drove me back down into the trees with crushing force, bouncing me halfway toward the forest floor. But I don't want to scare her with details. "I can see why ships choose not to land here."

I bring up my ICC, pleased I had the foresight to turn on my sensor before cresting the tree line. Jennifer leans close, trying to see the information. "I can't read it."

"Let me show you." I pull her onto my lap, showing her the symbols and graphs.

She's a quick learner, and soon has her phone in hand, adjusting the settings on her beacon. "This is exactly the information I needed."

I love how excited she is about her work. She could accomplish so much with the equipment my company could provide. I really hope we get rescued so I can be at her side while she explores the universe.

When she finishes with her phone, she sets it aside and gives me a naughty smirk. "Now we just need to wait for nightfall. Any thoughts on how we might kill some time?"

With a growl, I roll her onto her back among the leaves.

17

JENNIFER

Nazhin and I make love twice more while we wait for the daylight to fade, pausing only to snack on purple fruit and mushrooms. Eventually, the glow overhead deepens from pale pink to maroon, indicating darkness is coming. I set the phones in the center of the hollow.

"Here goes nothing," I say, and engage the beacon.

We wait a few minutes, as if expecting something to happen. When I realize I'm holding my breath, I let it out. "Well, that's it. All we can do now is wait. Do you think anyone is in orbit to hear it?"

Nazhin hugs me to his chest and sighs. "The real question is whether anyone will try to come for us if they do hear it. We've done everything *we* can to get off this planet."

I nod against his warmth. "At least we have each other now." I've thought a lot about our future. Whether we remain stranded here or not, I'm glad to have Nazhin at my side.

He kisses the top of my head. "We can face anything together, my *bareshi*."

I loop the strap of my messenger bag over my head. It feels strangely empty now. No phones. No equipment. Not even any food. "Let's get back to the others before we freeze to death."

Once again in my harness, I wrap my arms and legs around Nazhin as he jumps from our branch. The wind stings my skin and steals my breath, so I close my eyes as we dodge the massive limbs. When we reach the thickest layer, Nazhin resorts to hopping from branch to branch, sometimes walking along a limb before we can find a spot wide enough to squeeze through.

"I don't remember it being this difficult coming up," I say as we pause. The darkness here is eerie, and I glance around, worried something might be watching us.

"I think I'm just tired," he says.

Not wanting him to think I'm criticizing his efforts, I brush his lips in a kiss. "I think I'm just eager to be back. You're freaking amazing."

He kisses the tip of my nose. "Save the congratulations until after we get back safely."

His concern is unwarranted, and we soon clear the last of the massive, horizontal branches. Massive trunks still block most of the view, but I look down over the glowing neon colors of the understory while Nazhin glides between the trees. His wings tremble, and our course feels a little unstable. Plus, he's breathing hard.

Circling a massive trunk, he says, "I don't think we came down in the same spot."

Worry fills my gut, and I scan the ground below us, looking for any sign of the camp. Without our phones, we have no way to track each other. "How far off course might we be?"

"I'm not sure." He drops toward a pond, but there is no sign of a camp, so he pumps his wings to gain altitude again.

"Maybe we should land and rest," I suggest.

"No, I think I smell smoke," he says, looking around. "Can you tell where it's coming from?"

We circle a few more times before I spot a brighter glow among the bioluminescent foliage. I point. "There. I think that's our fire."

With stomach lurching speed, we drop to the clearing. People immediately gather around, and I see several unfamiliar faces crowding around. I pull the knot on my harness to free myself and proudly announce, "The beacon's set."

But this doesn't receive the hopeful response I expected. Instead, Tamara pushes past Erud with Beanie in her arms. Her eyes are puffy and her cheeks are red. "Oh, Jennifer!"

Concern flares in my chest. My sister has always been prone to anxiety, but something obviously happened while we were gone. "What is it?"

Her face creases with agony, and she chokes out, "Suzanne is missing."

I look around, realizing my oldest sister's strawberry blonde hair is nowhere in sight. "Have you looked for her?"

"Of course we looked for her." Tamara's voice is an octave too high. "She's gone. What if the parasite took her?"

"Or the Sheeghr?" Erud adds, his red mustache and eyebrows drawn into a tight scowl.

"Or one of those monsters with so many legs?" asks a Kirenai I don't recognize.

My stomach suddenly feels filled with rocks.

ear Reader,

Thanks for reading Nazhin and Jennifer's story. We'll be seeing them again in the next book featuring Suzanne and her "one-night-stand," Kiozhi, who, of course, turns out to be so much more. Join their steamy action as they try to protect the survivors from the horrors of the Singing Planet.

Knocked up at seventeen, I've spent more than half my life sacrificing for my family. Now I'm ready to have some fun. But this hot blue alien won't leave me alone...

Tap the cover to preorder your copy now!

Until next time!

Love, Tamsin

KIOZHI

SNEAK PEEK

KIOZHI

The moment I step onto the starship observation deck, my *Iki'i* is bombarded by the effervescent sensation of hundreds of emotions. This is the first night of the Intergalactic Dating Agency's inaugural cruise with human passengers, and the deck is packed, everyone bathed in an aurora of pastel colors from a nebula shining through the dome overhead. A small band plays on a stage in the center of the deck while people on the surrounding dance floor sway to the music.

Many of the females stand in small clusters surrounded by male suitors from every race across the galaxy. There are so many lovely shades of skin; deep brown, golden, and some who are as pale as starlight. The women all wear different fashions, from gauzy to svelte, though most seem to favor the color black, and the smells of so many perfumes are almost overwhelming.

A light-skinned female strides past me in a knee-length black dress with a cutout back panel that exposes the ridge of her spine. A unique hair clip with a spray of gems that look like stars holds her dark brown hair away from her face. I gaze after her appreciatively until a Kirenai following close on her heels with an enormous case in his arms glares at me, his aura radiating menace.

I understand immediately. It was that way with Nanaia when we met, an all-consuming desire that couldn't be ignored. The devastating accident that took her from me sent me into a depression that ruled my life for many cycles.

I jerk my attention away from the female walking past me. There are many other females available for my attention, and I wouldn't interfere with someone finding a mate. I'm not here to replace Nanaia—that would be impossible. Kirenai mate for life, and finding my true mate had been a one-in-a-million chance, anyway. But my body still has needs, and I can afford to treat any female who wishes to be with me like a princess.

I glance at my friend, Tazhio, next to me. He has the worried look of an old man who's lost his way. "You look like you could use a swig or ten of something strong," I say.

Tazhio nods and snags two glasses of Lensoran bubbly from a passing tray. "Got it covered."

He didn't want to be here tonight, but he's a good friend and agreed to be my *wingman,* a human term for one male who supports another during courting. Like me, he's Kirenai, but he's in his Hypawan form, which looks mostly human except for overly large eyes and very thick hair. As part of the crew, he wears a white uniform that stands out among the mostly black clothing worn by everyone else.

I smile, take the offered glass, then turn my attention back to the humans. My human-style finery—a "tux", the tailor called it—fits my current human form perfectly; broad shoulders, tall straight spine, muscular legs ending on flat feet. The IDA assured us this template is the most pleasing to human females, though I can adjust my features to please whichever woman I might choose for the evening.

A pretty brunette talking to several other women catches my eye. Her hair is piled on top of her head, cascading down in a mass of curls. Her lips have been painted with a glistening red substance that reminds me of fruit. A slit in her long black dress exposes a long length of golden thigh I'd love to explore further.

I step forward, running my gaze up and down her curves. "Hello, ma'am."

The woman turns to me with an assessing glance, eyes narrowed. "Ma'am? Do I look like a ma'am?"

The IDA told us we should use the term in polite human conversation. Apparently, they were wrong. "My apologies. I was informed the title was honorific. What shall I call you?"

"I'm Amanda, and this is Genevieve and Flora." She gestures toward a tall blonde and a petite brunette. They nod in greeting.

"I'm Kiozhi." I take her hand, turning her palm up to brush a kiss across her skin. A giddy thrill races through her at my touch, but she firmly pulls her hand free of my grip. I don't allow this to stop me—this is precisely why I brought a wingman. "This is my friend, Tazhio. As you can see, he's Kirenai too."

Tazhio is looking out at the crowd, not paying attention to the women at all. I elbow him and he jerks back, glancing at Amanda. "Oh, yes, greetings."

The women all giggle and nod appreciatively at him. I frown. Perhaps I shouldn't have brought a wingman after all.

"So," the other brunette drawls, "what are you two looking for in a woman?"

I shrug. "Tazhio's not allowed to date the passengers. But I would be happy to explore a night of pleasure with you."

She places a finger against her chin thoughtfully and looks me up and down again. "Oh, I bet you would," she says, her voice heavy with sarcasm. "But we're here looking for relationships, not one-night-stands."

I blink, not fully understanding her terminology. She seems to interpret my confusion as confirmation of her judgement and turns away. *Kuzara.* Finding companionship to ease my ever-present depression isn't going to be as quick and easy as I imagined.

I turn to Tazhio to complain and find him gone, disappeared somewhere into the crowd. I sigh. So much for my wingman.

On the dance floor, several beautiful women are moving to the music, laughing, flirting with their partners. I move forward to watch. Each female is divine in her own way, though I can't help comparing each one to my Nanaia and have to forcefully block her from my mind. I divert myself by imagining what it might be like to entwine myself with one of these females, to feel her body pressed against mine and our tongues dancing together in passion. Though my mate is gone, my sex drive is not, and providing pleasure gives me joy and helps keep my lingering depression at bay.

A laugh catches my attention. It reminds me of a clear waterfall chiming against the crystal cliffs on my home planet of Alkavar III. *Who is that?* Suddenly, I want to be the one making her laugh.

Intrigued, I follow the sound and discover a female with ivory skin and the most delightful shade of hair I've ever encountered—a light red-gold that reminds me of a sunset. She's twirling across the dance floor in the arms of a Kirenai my *Iki'i* doesn't recognize. Her short black dress is covered in what look like small scales that catch the light with pearly iridescence. The glimmer accentuates her curves in a way that makes my heart pound faster.

She spins past me, brilliant green eyes connecting with mine for an instant. My mating shaft stirs, a long-forgotten ache flaring low in my belly. I stumble back in confusion. I haven't felt this sensation since Nanaia died.

The female tosses her hair and looks away, an amused grin on her face as the other male guides her across the dance floor. Normally, I'd approach her without hesitation, but after my last interaction, I need to understand what's happening first. I push through the crowd to keep up with her, just a shadow in the distance. My breathing quickens as I watch her hips sway. I feel like a youth again, eager and impulsive. She's mine, I know it. I must win her away from this other male.

SUZANNE

I tip my head back and laugh as I spin across the dance floor in the arms of yet another tall blue alien. So far, I've danced with at least six hot guys, with more lined up for a chance to swing me off my feet. Tonight is the first night of our singles cruise, and I made a promise to myself that I wouldn't dance with the same guy twice, at least not on the first night. After seventeen years trapped in a horrible marriage, I'm finally free. I haven't had this much fun since getting knocked up in high school, and I'm determined to make the most of this two-week singles cruise through space.

The song ends, and I snag a glass of whatever this stuff is that passes for alien champagne from a passing server's tray. "I need to catch my breath," I tell my dance partner.

He doesn't look like he wants to let me go, but I flit away before he can protest, ducking behind a couple doing a wild approximation of swing dancing. The room is filled with all sorts of aliens, from handsome blue Kirenai with action figure bodies to short, frail-looking Area 51 beings with gray-green skin and huge dark eyes.

Overhead, multicolored ribbons of light and thousands of glittering stars illuminate the domed ceiling. I move back toward where I left my sisters at the edge of the dance floor, sipping the bubbly, fruity drink and smiling at every hot alien who glances my direction. I know I look good in my silky black cocktail dress with rose-gold sequins that match my hair. All around me is laughter and talking in a hundred different languages. I'm still wrapping my head around the fact I can understand them all—alien and human alike—thanks to a translator implant I get to keep when the trip is over. Maybe I'll use it to land a job as a corporate translator when I get back to Earth. Wouldn't that be something?

I pass by a hulking gray dude with wings, horns, and a tail who gives me a once-over before breaking into a sharp-toothed grin. Although he's got a rocking bod, his features are a bit too gargoyle for my taste, and he carries himself like he knows what he wants. It's that last part that I turn away from. I've had enough of men who bully me to get what they want.

When I discovered I was pregnant, Robbie insisted we get married. Then he convinced me to work as a bank teller to put him through medical school after the twins were born. It felt like we were always waiting for that next step when life would come together. Less than a year ago, just before the kids graduated high school, he asked for a divorce. Turns out he was seeing a younger, hotter version of me and got her pregnant. Now he "has a responsibility to take care of his family"—with the medical practice I helped him build. *Fucking bastard.*

This cruise with my sisters is my new start. My "Hot Girl Sumer." The taste of freedom I never had.

I dodge another alien who's looking at me with a proprietary gaze and search for my sisters. I want to see if they're having fun, too. Lifting my chin, I locate my sister, Jennifer fiddling with her telescope at one edge of the observation deck. She's insisting on using this trip to gather astronomy data for her doctoral thesis and is somehow successfully ignoring the constant stream of alien men asking her to dance. It probably helps that the tall, bald Kirenai who's been hauling her equipment around glares daggers at anyone who comes near.

I'd prefer not to be dragged into one of my brainy sister's dissertations about random star systems, so I keep looking. I spot Tamara's copper curls through the crowd. It looks like she's heading to the dance floor with a red-skinned alien who reminds me of a dwarf from Lord of the Rings. *Good for her.* She's usually so shy, I'm glad to see she's having fun.

That leaves our youngest sister, Bethany. I know just where to look for her—near the kitchen, stalking an alien chef she wants to host on her cooking show. Spotting her in her deep wine-colored cocktail dress, I swoop over and take her hand. "God, I'm having such a good time. Take a break and dance with me."

"Stop, Suzanne." She yanks her hand away, planting it back on her hip. "There's a Nebula Chef on board, and I'm waiting to speak with him. I wish they'd just let me go talk to him in the kitchen."

I sigh. Getting an alien on her show will probably send her ratings to the top, but this is a once in a lifetime trip, and all she can think about is her job. I examine the alien appetizers on a nearby table and pick up something that looks exactly like a small red penis. "Maybe they're not letting you in the kitchen because they don't want you to know their alien dicks aren't fresh."

One of the small Area 51-looking servers stumbles slightly, obviously overhearing me. I flash him a naughty grin, sure his cheeks turn pink underneath all that gray skin before he turns and scurries away. I sniff the little dick, wrinkling my nose at the musty odor, then shove it under Bethany's nose. "You try one of these yet?"

“This is serious.” She scowls, shoving my hand away. "Besides, You're the only one who insisted this trip was all about meeting hot aliens. Go dance with one of them." Bethany gestures toward a nearby Kirenai.

Most of the Kirenai look similar, but there's something about this one that makes my engine rev. Perhaps it's the magnetism of his midnight dark eyes. I'm not sure if I've danced with him before, but damn, he's hot enough I might consider a second turn around the dance floor, promise to myself be damned.

He moves forward and holds out a hand. “I noticed you from across the room.” His rumbling voice cuts below the music and makes my delicate parts tingle. Ok, I don’t think I’ve danced with him because I would’ve remembered that voice. "Would you care to dance?"

“Sure.” I shrug, trying not to appear eager as I start past him toward the dance floor.

He stops me with an arm around my waist. Pulling me closer, he starts to sway to the music. Maybe it’s the slightly crooked way he smiles, or the subtle, almost chocolatey scent of his cologne, but I find myself nodding and looping my arms around his neck. "Something wrong with the dance floor?"

Guiding me in time to the music, he leans close to my ear. "There are too many people there. I want you all to myself."

Oh, boy. That deep voice really makes my girly parts flutter. I’ve never had a one-night-stand, but I’m starting to think tonight is the night. It’s a big step for me. *You are allowed to have fun.* I repeat the mantra my therapist gave me. Tilting my head back, I meet his gaze. "That's hard to do in a room full of people."

Gaze still connected, he pulls me more firmly against him. Heat pools between my legs as I recognize the throbbing length now trapped between our bodies. "Yes, very hard."

I don't even know his name, but I don't care. I close the distance between our lips. His arms fold around me like a cloak as his kiss ravages my mouth. His fingers toy with the hair at the base of my neck, sending shivers down my spine. I wrap both arms around his ribs and let my hands play up and down the broad muscles of his back. Our tongues tangle until I've lost all sense of space and time.

I'm panting with desire and my nipples ache inside my dress by the time he pauses. I want him to touch me, to love me, to make me whole again. Voice raspy with need, I ask, "Should we take this back to your room or mine?"

I hope you enjoyed seeing how Suzanne and Kiozhi met! You'll get to see how they reach their happily-ever-after in the next book, KIOZHI. It hits the bookstores on October 31, so be sure you don't miss it and preorder your copy now!

PREORDER KIOZHI

GLOSSARY

Bacca - a game that resembles frisbee golf.

Bareshi - brilliant one.

Burendo - a Kirenai who excels at shapeshifting and is able to not only assume the form of other species, but coloration as well.

Fogarian - aliens with red hair and sideburns who live on a rocky, mountainous planet.

G'nax - a species that uses light to communicate attraction and arousal. They also have a symbiotic relationship with an eight-legged insectoid.

Hage - bald, wide-eyed alien that looks much like the iconic alien humans have circulated.

Happa trees - blue fronds resembling palms.

Hypawa - species with magma colored eyes.

ICC - Integrated Circuit Chip - an embedded chip that is an alien version of a holographic smart phone

Ijin'en - four legged herd animal raised for meat and well known for its stupidity.

Iki'i - empathic power.

Irn - a unit of measure. One planetary rotation around the Kirenai's sun.

Jiro - a unit of measure equivalent to approximately two Earth hours.

K'ogai - the town near the palace on Kirenai Prime.

Kazhitu - nuts that look like sticky buns when baked. High in sugar, buttery and fruity.

Khargals - gray horned aliens with stone-like skin and wings from the planet Duras ;)

Khensei - a toxin that causes Kirenai to denature into their resting state.

Kikajiru - my distracting one - a term of endearment.

Kirenai Prime - the Kirenai home planet. Purple and blue with swirling white clouds.

Kuzara - shit, damn, fuck.

Kryillian death swarm - tiny insectoid creatures that can kill a man within seconds by sucking his blood.

Lensoran bubbly - alien champagne

Lonala moth - fragile insect native to Hypawa

Malila flowers - fragrant, night-blooming flowers popular in conservatories across the galaxy

Matrix/cellular matrix - the term for a Kirenai's cellular mass.

Nilgawood - a tree used to make resin.

Oritsu - An expression of awe.

Popotan - the plant used to line ship interiors that provides oxygen, recycles water, is highly resistant to radiation, and can regenerate itself if damaged.

Qalqan - a species known for their healers. Good bedside manners due to their resistance to emotional fluctuation.

Resting state - a Kirenai's amorphous shape, like nakedness to humans, it is shown only to family or trusted friends.

Senburu - a galactic conglomeration of merchants who oppose the emperor's rule. Individual members are called *Senbur.*

Sireta Prime - a popular party planet.

Sowain - tastes like chicken!

Supo cloth - smart fabric for clothing that doesn't need buttons or zippers.

Teozhisa - a cart to carry people.

Tolonovone - a device that creates lighted markings on the skin. Used by G'naxians as part of their mating rituals.

Ukimi ice - beloved dessert with cool, spicy flavor like sweet mint.

Urru - purple egg-sized fruits from the Singing Planet that taste like cantaloupe

Vatosangans - species with alabaster skin and blue or green hair who tend to be stocky or rounded. Planet is called Vatosang.

KIRENAI FACT SHEET

Kirenai are an all-male species of shapeshifters with a natural form (resting state) like an amoeba who usually assume a bipedal shape to interact with other species. Until the discovery of humans, Kirenai required a permanent pair-bond with a female of another species to produce offspring. All Kirenai traits are dominant and located on the Y chromosome; male offspring are fully Kirenai, while female offspring are fully of the mother's species.

Birth rates have been historically low, and over the ages, the population has dwindled. Human females are exceptionally receptive to impregnation, and do not require formation of a pair-bond to conceive, which has made Earth a target for black market slave traders who deal in "breeders." The Emperor is making attempts to protect the population.

Regardless of the shape a Kirenai's matrix is in, he cannot change his skin or hair color. The most common color is blue, although hues range anywhere from mint green to lavender. Rare individuals, called *burendo,* can vary coloration outside this range. Kirenai blood is clear or slightly milky unless infected, when it grows murky to almost solid white.

All Kirenai have empathic abilities called *Iki'i* which make them capable of reading emotion and desire, and also enables them to identify individuals within their own species regardless of shape. This is the only Kirenai trait sometimes passed on to female progeny. The ability also makes the species consummate lovers because they can take actions and form attributes their partner finds most appealing. Bonded mates assume a permanent form pleasing to their mates; rarely can they force themselves into an alternate shape after bonding.

The average Kirenai life-span is approximately eight hundred human years. When a pair-bond is formed, a Kirenai passes a small genetic market to his mate that mitigates the aging process, giving the mate a lifespan to match his own.

OTHER GALACTIC RACES

Qalqan – A pink, lizard-like race who are innately skilled at medicine. They have more than two genders and change genders as they age, which makes reproduction rather complex. It also means means they rarely pair-bond with Kirenai. In addition, their emotions are hard to understand for others and unreadable by Kirenai *iki'i*.

Hypawa – A race with large, expressive eyes, smooth luminescent skin, and luscious hair on their heads and eyelashes; considered by many to be the most beautiful race in the galaxy. Their origin is a mystery - even their supposed world of origin doesn't seem to be their homeworld. Their economy is dependent on tourism and entertainment.

G'nax – A spiny, bug-like race that can breathe a variety of atmospheres. Biologically they are inclined to be traders and have senses that let them navigate through hyperspace. They use light to communicate attraction and arousal. The females have a symbiotic relationship with an eight-legged insectoid which secretes dew used to feed G'naxian infants.

Khargal – A horned, gray-skinned race that can enter a hybernating state where their body becomes stonelike. The number of horns indicates the amount of royal blood in them. Honor is more important to them than anything. They have wings and claws and resemble gargoyles of Earth mythology. Their planet of origin is a barren world that has two moons and is known for having some unusual ore deposits and relatively few life forms.

Fogarian – A burly, thick-skinned race with crimson hair, claws, and fangs. They come from a high-gravity planet rich in crystalline gemstones and excel at digging. The females usually bear litters of two to four offspring, and are favored mates for Kirenai. Fogarians tend to be very straightforward and keep their promises, even if it means death.

Vatosangan – A small, slight race with alabaster skin, rounded features, and blue to black hair. As the most common race to pair-bond with Kirenai, some say they actually control the galactic empire behind the scenes. They seek any alliance, technology, or advantage that will benefit them, and their current government is a meritocracy.

Klen – A green-skinned humanoid race with eyes on extendable stalks. Their tongues can act as prehensile limbs, and they have the ability to withstand a wide range of temperatures. They are a race of scavengers and can modify some of their bodily secretions to become various useful substances.

Hage – Short, bald, gray-skinned aliens with large heads. They were the first to make contact with humans. Though their scrawny frame doesn't suggest it, they are addicted to the pleasures of taking nutrition, and their cuisine is spectacular. A past war obliterated their homeworld, and they now live scattered among the other races, usually employed in a service capacity.

Sheeghr – Not advanced enough to be admitted to the Galactic Confederation. A matriarchal, ferret-like race native to the Singing Planet. Known for hypersexuality, the females maintain a constant state of pregnancy to ward off a native parasite called a Gloor. Any female who refuses or who cannot get pregnant is killed. The males determine rank based on the size and color of their phalluses.

Human – New members the Galactic Confederation. This bipedal race has not yet homogenized into a single language, culture or appearance. The species has skin tones that vary between black and alabaster, with shades of brown in between. The females are capable of reproducing with many other species throughout the galaxy, and have become a target for illegal slave trading.

INTERGALACTIC DATING AGENCY

Looking for more out of this world romance? Your local Intergalactic Dating Agency can help! These strong, smart, sexy aliens are on the prowl for mates, and humans like you are exactly what they're after. Jump in with Book 1 of any standalone trilogy from our crew of rock star SFR authors and make steamy first contact! Warning: abductions may or may not be included!

Grab more hunky alien action here:

http://romancingthealien.com

ALSO BY TAMSIN LEY

Galactic Pirate Brides series

Rescued by Qaiyaan

Ransomed by Kashatok

Claimed by Noatak

Taken by the Cyborg

Mates for Monsters

The Merman's Kiss

The Merman's Quest

A Mermaid's Heart

The Centaur's Bride

The Djinn's Desire

Khargals of Duras

Sticks and Stones

Alaska Alphas

Alpha Origins

Untamed Instinct

Bewitched Shifter

Midnight Heat

Wild Child

Kirenai Fated Mates (Intergalactic Dating Agency)

Arazhi

Zhiruto

Iroth

****POST-APOCALYPTIC SCIENCE FICTION WRITTEN AS TAM LINSEY****

Botanicaust

The Reaping Room

Doomseeds

Amarantox

ABOUT THE AUTHOR

Once upon a time I thought I wanted to be a biomedical engineer, but experimenting on lab rats doesn't always lead to happy endings. Now I blend my nerdy infatuation of science with character-driven romance and guaranteed happily-ever-afters. My monsters always find their mates, with feisty heroines, tortured heroes, and all the steamy trouble they can handle. I promise my stories will never leave you hanging (although you may still crave more!)

When I'm not writing, I'll be in the garden or the kitchen, exploring Alaska with my husband, or preparing for the zombie apocalypse. I also love wine and hard apple cider, my noisy chickens, and attempting to crochet.

Interested in more about me? Join my VIP Club and get free books, notices, and other cool stuff!

www.tamsinley.com

BB bookbub.com/authors/tamsin-ley
g goodreads.com/TamsinLey
f facebook.com/TamsinLey
instagram.com/tamsinley
tiktok.com/@tamsinley?
a amazon.com/author/tamsin

Made in the USA
Las Vegas, NV
14 December 2023

82733985R00105